SUMMER REFRESH

JENNIFER FAYE

LAZY DAZY PRESS

CONTENTS

ABOUT THIS BOOK...

With a housing shortage on the island, making a deal with the man who broke her sister's heart becomes the only way to reunite her family.

Sara Chen enjoys working at the Brass Anchor Inn and hopes to be promoted to manager. And so when the inn's new owner goes on vacation, it's Sara's chance to step up and impress her boss while doing whatever is necessary to help her sister move back to the island—even if it includes dealing with a man from her past.

Kent Turner works in his family's furniture business, but he feels stifled. Every new idea he has to expand the business is shot down. Wanting to do more than the finances, he decides to put one of his ideas into action. He starts a refresh project at the local inn.

But with a big wedding coming up, the project has to be done quickly. It will mean hiring help...unless he makes a deal with the beautiful yet stubborn inn employee. If she'll help him complete the refresh project, he'll rent the apartment above the furniture store to her sister. But as they work together, secrets are revealed, relationships are given a second chance, and love is found.

Includes a recipe for Sara's apricot blondie bars!

Bluestar Island series:

Book 1 – Love Blooms (Hannah & Ethan)

Book 2 – Harvest Dance (Aster & Sam)

Book 3 – A Lighthouse Café Christmas (Darla & Will)

Book 4 – Rising Star (Emma & Noah)

Book 5 – Summer by the Beach (Summer & Greg)

Book 6 – Brass Anchor Inn (Josie & Lane)

Book 7 – Summer Refresh (Sara & Kent)

Book 8 – A Seaside Bookshop Christmas (Melinda & Liam)

CHAPTER ONE

"**P**LEASE. I NEED YOU to do this."

Friday afternoon, Sara Chen stood behind the registration desk of Bluestar Island's most popular inn. She was the front desk clerk of the Brass Anchor Inn, with hopes of being promoted to manager. She held the phone to her ear, listening to her older sister's plea.

"Can't you just call Kent yourself?" Sara struggled to keep her voice low.

She couldn't believe her older sister was so desperate that she'd be willing to rent an apartment from the man who'd broken Cari's heart. Even though it'd happen a while ago, interactions with Kent Turner remained awkward.

"I tried," Cari said. "The number I have for him has been disconnected."

"Well, try the furniture store."

"I did. He wasn't in the office. It might be easier with the time difference if you talked to him."

Sara sighed. "Cari, I don't want to get in the middle of this."

"Please... I need your help. I've tried everyone I can think of to get a place to stay on the island, and Kent is my last hope."

"Besides, I don't think the units above the furniture store are short-term rentals."

"Just try. Please."

Sara's body stiffened as a tug of war waged within her. She wanted to help her sister. Really she did. But the last thing she wanted to do was to go to Kent and ask him for a favor. And yet she owed her older sister so much.

Sara sighed. "What makes you think Kent will be able to help you?"

"Well, Agnes Dewey told Peggy Weston, who told Sally Nash that one of the units over the furniture store was going to be available by the end of this month."

The gossip mill in Bluestar was definitely alive and well. The island was crescent-shaped and sat not far off the coast of Massachusetts. And summertime was their busiest season. If you didn't have reservations months in advance, you were out of luck. Even the Brass Anchor Inn was booked until September.

Sara rolled her eyes. "If that's the case, what makes you think they don't already have someone lined up to take the unit?"

Cari sighed. "I don't. But I hope it's still available because I... I'm coming home." There was a pause. "To stay."

Had she heard her sister correctly? Or was it just wishful thinking on her part. "Really?"

"Yes, really. I've missed you. And I've been gone too long."

The thought of having her sister back on the island permanently filled Sara with happiness. She couldn't think of anything she would like better. And with both of their parents gone, Cari was her only family. Thankfully, the small community on the island was a lot like family—a gossipy family but family all the same.

Cari had traveled for a while before taking a teaching position in Malaysia for the past couple of years. With the great distance and expense of traveling, she hadn't seen her sister in a few years. And she missed her so much. Phones were nice, but they just couldn't take the place of face-to-face conversations.

She also owed her sister for helping to raise her after their mother died when Sara was twelve. Their father had done his best, but their mother's absence left him deeply depressed. He'd submerged himself in his work at the docks until a heart attack stole him away when Sara was twenty-one.

A couple of years later, Sara and her sister had decided to sell the family home. It was too big for just the two of them. In all honesty, Sara never wanted to sell, but she knew her sister did, and after all Cari had done for her, she'd reluctantly agreed to the sale.

They'd split the money. Cari had paid off her student loans and used the rest of her money to see the world, or at least some of it. After paying her bills, Sara placed the rest of her money in the bank and tried to use as little of it as possible. It was her nest egg—her emergency fund.

After Cari left Bluestar, Sara had never felt more alone. And so, if this was what it took to get Cari home, then she would do it.

With hesitation, Sara said, "I'll do it because I love you."

"Thank you." The joy rang out in her sister's voice. "I owe you big time."

"Yes, you do. Just wait until you find out what it's going to cost." She let out an ominous laugh.

There was a slight pause. "And what's it going to cost me?"

"I don't know yet." Just then one of the inn's guests headed in Sara's direction with an expectant look on their face. Right behind them was her boss, Josie Turner. "Cari, I have to go back to work."

"Okay. But talk to Kent today before someone else scoops up the place."

"I will. I will. Love you."

"Love you too."

As Sara slipped her phone into her pocket, she smiled. Nothing could be better than having her sister home again. If only she didn't have to deal with Kent.

She pushed aside her problem and took care of the inn's guest. She pointed the person in the direction of The Bluff's restaurant and then turned to Josie, who was typing on the computer used for registrations. "Shouldn't you be on your way to the airport?"

Josie shook her head. "I've got too much to do here."

Wait. Was Josie saying she wasn't going to California to visit with her hunky boyfriend? That couldn't be right. Just yesterday Josie had been so excited about seeing where Lane lived. What had happened between then and now?

She watched as her boss logged into the airline website. "Are you canceling your trip?"

Josie shrugged as she continued to type. Her silence spoke volumes, and Sara grew worried.

She briefly placed a hand on Josie's arm. "What's the matter? Are you and Lane fighting?"

Josie stopped typing and looked at her. "No. It's nothing like that."

Sara looked into her troubled eyes. "What's it like then?"

For a moment, there was silence. "It's this place. I just worry about being so far away. In two weeks we have the Carrington wedding."

"And we've gone over the plans in great detail. I've got this." And then she realized the real problem. "You don't trust me, do you?"

Josie's hands withdrew from the keyboard. She turned to Sara. "That's not true. I have great confidence in you. Otherwise, I wouldn't have bought the airline tickets."

Sara wanted to believe her, but Josie's actions spoke louder than her words. "You might have the tickets, but you aren't planning to use them. Instead of spending the next two weeks with your good-looking boyfriend, you're going to stay here and do the same old same old."

Josie smiled. "He is good-looking, isn't he?"

Sara nodded. "But you'll have to stare at his picture on your phone, since you aren't going to see him in person."

Josie paused to consider things. "I do really miss him."

"And I'm certain he misses you too."

She sighed. "It's just so hard to leave here. I worry about things."

"But see, that's the thing. With Harvey and I taking care of everything here, there's nothing for you to worry about."

Josie smiled and nodded. "I know."

"Then what are you doing standing here? You have a ferry to catch to the mainland so you don't miss your plane."

Josie glanced at her smart watch. "I better hurry."

"Go. I've got this."

"Thank you." Josie gave her a hug and then rushed off.

Sara was happy for Josie and Lane. They made a perfect couple. She was also looking forward to this opportunity to prove herself. Nothing would go wrong while Josie was gone. Not a thing.

If only her conversation with Kent wasn't hanging over her head. He didn't like her any more than she liked him. Of course, she might have instigated the mutual ill will in a misguided attempt to protect her sister.

On that long ago summer, Kent had dated her sister for months, and then suddenly he stood Cari up for their cousin's wedding. No phone call. No explanation. He was just gone. Cari had been so upset that she wouldn't speak of it.

Sara had sought him out at his parents' furniture store. She wasn't about to let him treat her sister that way. When she asked him why he'd dumped her sister and he wouldn't answer, she told him he was an unfeeling jerk and a few other things. Unfortunately for both of them, the outburst took place in front of his parents and some customers. It definitely wasn't her finest moment.

At the time, she'd told herself she was defending her sister—just like her sister had done for her ever since their mother died. But all of these years later, she wondered if it was more than that. Had she taken her anger over her mother's death out on him?

She hadn't taken their mother's death well. She'd acted out at school—fighting with anyone that even looked at her. She had been so full of anger over the unfairness of it all. And her father had seemed to check out of life.

Ever since then, there had been a distinct chilliness between her and Kent. She didn't know how she was supposed to convince him to rent the apartment to her sister, but she would give it her best effort.

Chapter Two

W HAT WAS IT GOING to take?

Kent Turner sighed as he stood in the office of Turner Home Furnishings. He'd been having a meeting with his parents to discuss expanding the services of the furniture store. It wasn't his first time to have this conversation. Over the last couple of years, he'd proposed various ideas from patio furniture to lighting fixtures.

This time he'd come to the meeting with a slideshow presentation with graphs and charts. They smiled and nodded. They told him how proud they were of him. For just a moment, he thought he had finally sold them on his vision.

His parents' response was the same as it had been in the past: why change what works? Frustration had balled up in his gut. He tried to tell them that it was what they had to do if they wanted to grow. They didn't seem interested in growth. They were content with their steady business as they were the only furniture store on the island.

Once again, they told him how proud they were of him and what a professional presentation he'd made. In the next breath, they told him the venture was too risky. Now that they were looking ahead to retirement, they didn't want to take any chances.

And that was it. No further conversation. No nothing.

For a while now, he'd been considering that he just didn't fit into the vision his parents had for the business. Perhaps it was time he moved on just as his siblings had done. It was a thought that tempted and teased him.

Still the thought of leaving the island—of leaving his family and friends—well, it was a daunting thought. Perhaps he was more set in his ways than he'd thought. Still, he couldn't just give up trying to have a bigger role in this business or perhaps another business.

He had a couple of weeks of vacation time starting tomorrow. He would use that time to figure out where he went from here. He couldn't just keep settling.

"I'm sorry, Kent," his mother said. "It truly does sound like a good idea, but we're just not in a place to take on risky ideas right now. I hope you understand." She made her way out of the office.

Once his mother was gone, Kent turned his attention to his father. "Do you agree with her?"

His dad didn't immediately respond. "You have to understand that at our stage in life, we don't want to take any risks."

"But without risk, there's no chance for growth."

"I understand. Really I do. And when this business is yours, you can do with it as you please."

"But when will that be?"

His father's bushy brows rose. "Well... Uh, I don't know exactly."

"This year? Next year?"

His father frowned. "Are you that anxious to push us out the door?"

"It's not like that and you know it. After working here for years, I just need to feel like part of the business is mine too."

"But it is. Your name is on the door."

"No. That's the family name."

A long awkward pause ensued. Kent didn't like being at odds with his parents, but being amenable wasn't getting him any closer to his goals. If it were up to his parents, nothing would ever change with the business.

"Maybe the vacation will do you good." His father had a hopeful look on his face. "We can talk when you get back."

And then he had to say the one thing that he'd been dreading. "You should probably know that I'm considering leaving the business...and the island."

His father didn't look surprised in the least. It was as though his father had suspected something like this. "I hope it doesn't come to that, but if it's what you need to do to be happy, then we'll understand."

He knew his dad was trying to smooth things over, but this wasn't the first time they'd had this conversation, and it never changed—they never changed. And Kent knew he was too young to just do the same old thing for the rest of his life. He wanted to try new things and take risks.

He also understood where his parents were coming from, but it didn't make it any better for him. No matter how many times he asked them about the future, he never got a definitive answer. And now he had to make one for himself.

Selling furniture was great, and they were doing well, but he needed to put his own mark on the business. His latest proposal was to add a decorating service. He even had a name for the service—Refresh.

He didn't have to tie the decorating service into the furniture business, even though they would dovetail together nicely. Perhaps he should give this side business a try. After all, he had the next two weeks to do as he pleased. He could use that time to see if this was an avenue he wanted to go down. He liked to paint, and he was good with furniture placement. What more was there to it?

"I'm leaving early today," Kent told his father. "Can you close up?"

"Sure. No problem." His father glanced up from where he was attaching a sales tag to one of the newly delivered couches. "Are you stopping by the house for dinner tonight?"

Kent enjoyed his mother's cooking and the free food, but tonight he had other plans. "I don't think I'll make it tonight."

"Are you sure? Your mother is making her homemade macaroni and cheese."

It was one of his favorite dishes, and his father knew it. "Sounds good, but I can't make it."

Kent went over some items that would need to be addressed while he was out of the office. Once his father had a list of the open items, Kent made his way out the door.

In his rush to put his newly formed plan into motion, he almost ran into someone. "Sorry."

He lifted his head and came face-to-face with Sara Chen. Her straight dark hair was cut short, and her olive complexion was flawless. Her big brown eyes had flecks of gold in them, and they were framed by long dark lashes. Her small nose led to her heart-shaped mouth.

He swallowed hard. How was it possible that every time he saw her, she grew more beautiful? Finding himself staring at her, he glanced away.

He gave himself a mental shake. It didn't matter how beautiful he found her, she was the last person he should be attracted to. She'd made her dislike for him well-known some time ago. Since then she'd kept her distance from him. Even when she needed furniture, she made sure to come to the store when he wasn't there. He couldn't prove that she did it intentionally, but he had his suspicions.

Sara sent him a hesitant smile. "No problem."

"Excuse me." He went to go around her.

She stepped to the side, right in his path. "Actually, you're the person I need to see."

"Me?" His voice came out an octave higher than normal. Immediately, he assumed she wanted to order furniture. "Listen, if this is about placing an order, you'll have to see my father. He's inside."

He stepped around her and kept going. When Sara rushed around the front of his cart and sat down next to him, he was surprised.

She gave him a pointed look. "This is really important."

"I don't have time now. I have an appointment." He looked at her, expecting her to get out of the cart.

She didn't make any motion to move. "We can talk on the way."

Surely he hadn't heard her correctly, but when he started the cart, she still refused to move. "You don't even know where I'm going."

She shrugged. "It doesn't matter. This is a small island. You can't take me anywhere that I can't walk home."

He frowned at her. He wasn't used to Sara being so pushy. In fact, except for that one time a long time ago, she was normally reserved around him. "You aren't going to get out, are you?"

She shook her head and crossed her arms.

He let out another sigh as he stepped on the accelerator. He had to admit he was curious about what was so urgent that it had Sara acting out of character. However, as he drove, he noticed she didn't say anything. He cleared his throat as though to get her attention, but she still didn't speak.

He glanced over at her. "Sara, what did you need to talk to me about?"

"What's the deal with you and my sister?"

His back teeth ground together. This was one subject he didn't discuss with anyone. "There's no deal. I haven't seen her in a long time."

"She said she tried to call you, but you were dodging her calls."

"I was not." The denial came out a little too quickly. He swallowed. "I didn't even know she wanted to speak to me." He could see the disbelief reflected in Sara's eyes. "It's true." He regretted those last two words as soon as he'd uttered them. They just made it sound like he wasn't telling the truth.

What was it about being around Sara that rattled him? Yes, she was pretty, but he'd been around other pretty women, and they hadn't gotten him tripping over his own tongue. But then again none were as good-looking as Sara. Not that he was interested in her or anything.

He slowed the cart to a stop. "If all you want to do is talk about the past, you might as well get out here."

"It's not." Her answer was uttered too quickly.

"Then what did you need? You're running out of time."

"It made it through the grapevine that you have an apartment over the store that's going to be available soon."

Above the furniture store were six apartments. Renting them out fell under his responsibilities at the store. It wasn't hard because it was rare for any of the units to be vacant. Basically, he collected the rent and issued lease renewals. Easy-peasy.

He pressed on the accelerator again. "You want to rent an apartment?"

She shrugged. "Do you have one available?"

"I will at the end of the month."

"That's great!" The smile returned to her face.

He felt as though she was up to something. He just had no idea what it was. "But don't you already have an apartment?"

She nodded. "I...I do."

"Then why do you want a two-bedroom apartment?"

She glanced away. Silence engulfed them as they made their way through town. People waved, and they both waved back. A couple of people did a double-take at seeing the two of them together. He inwardly groaned. Just what he needed was for the town to gossip about a blooming romance between him and Sara. That was never going to happen.

"Maybe I want to move." Sara avoided meeting his gaze.

He sensed she was holding something back. Why would a single woman want a two-bedroom apartment that costs a lot more than a single or studio? He thought about it as the cart moved north of the town.

Was it possible she was being evicted from her current place? Sara a troublemaker? *Nah*. It didn't seem right to him.

Sure, there had been that one embarrassing incident when she'd accused him of something he hadn't done, but there were extenuating circumstances. Sara had been protecting her sister. And he'd never heard one bad word about Sara. In fact, the people on the island loved her.

Perhaps she was getting a roommate. Or maybe she was in a serious relationship. A sour feeling settled in the pit of his stomach. Kent yanked his rambling thoughts to a halt. His body jerked forward, jarring him back to the present.

"What's the matter?" The worry in Sara's voice had him glancing at her.

It was only then he realized that not only had he halted his thoughts, but he'd also slammed the break on the cart. Feeling utterly flustered, he turned away and pressed the accelerator. "I thought I saw something in the road."

"Oh." Thankfully, she left the conversation there. "So what do you say? Will you rent me the apartment?"

"I don't think it's a good idea."

"Listen, I know we haven't exactly gotten along in the past, but that was a long time ago."

The more she pushed the subject, the more concerned he became about her. It wasn't like they were friends, but that didn't mean he couldn't be concerned, especially with her sister so far away.

"So will you rent it to me?"

"No, I won't." He wasn't desperate to rent the place. The supply of available units was never adequate enough to meet the demand, especially in the summer months. He could afford to be picky.

"Why not?"

He stopped the cart in the inn's parking lot. "I think the less we have to do with each other the better."

Her frown turned into a glare. "I don't know why you have to be so stubborn." She stepped out of the cart. "Surely there has to be something we can work out?"

He shook his head. "No."

With a huff, she turned. Her shoulders were rigid as she made her way up the walk. He should turn away, but there was something about Sara that always intrigued him. Not that he ever had the chance to know her very well.

When they were in school, he'd been a few years ahead of her and they hadn't run in the same circles. He'd graduated with her sister, Cari. For a while their class had remained good friends after high school, including him and Cari. Sara had been too young for him. And then there was the incident with Cari. Ever since then she'd acted like she hated him. The truth of the matter was that he hadn't done anything wrong. Not that Sara would believe him, even if he had told her. But he'd made a promise. And he kept his word...even if the promise had been made many years ago.

CHAPTER THREE

THAT MAN.

Sara strode into the lobby of the inn. She wasn't sure why she'd stepped inside. It wasn't like she had to go back to work. Thankfully, her work day was over.

Harvey Coleman glanced up from the reception desk. He wore a dark blue polo shirt with the inn's logo embroidered with white thread. His snow-white hair was kept short as was his mustache and beard. He reminded her of Santa Claus. Instead of delivering gifts once a year to all the nice children, he was the inn's night manager, but with Josie out of town, he stepped up to take over the evening shift.

"Did you forget something?" His blue eyes sent her a puzzled look from behind his gold-rimmed glasses.

"I..." What did she say? That Kent got her so worked up she wasn't paying attention to where she went as long as it was away from him? No. "I just wanted to make sure I told you about the Weston's anniversary dinner this evening."

He nodded. "You did three times now. I'm old, but my memory still works."

"Sorry. I just have a lot on my mind." And right now she was letting down her sister. "Hey, you wouldn't know of anyone renting out an apartment on the island, would you?"

Harvey paused as though to give the question some thought. "No, I don't. But if I hear of one, you'll be the first person I tell." He arched a bushy white brow. "Are you planning to move?"

"Maybe." She didn't know why she was hesitant to tell people about her sister moving home. Maybe it was the fact that she was afraid to get her hopes up until Cari was on the island with her suitcase in hand.

It seemed as though all the people she loved were always leaving her. Maybe that was why she'd never had a serious romantic relationship. Maybe she mentally knew they would leave her sooner or later. It was easier to put up roadblocks than to get her heart broken.

When she didn't immediately move back toward the door, Harvey said, "If you're looking for something to do, I'm sure I can find you something."

She looked at him and smiled. "You sound much too eager to share your work."

"Can't blame a fella for trying."

"No, you can't. But since you have the Weston dinner under control, I think I'll head out again. Hope you have a good evening. And if you need anything, just let me know."

"I'm sure it'll be quiet." He sent her a reassuring look. "Have a good evening."

"Thanks." She moved back to the door.

She squinted in the late afternoon sun. Once her vision adjusted, she was surprised to find Kent's cart still there, but he was nowhere in sight. She wondered where he might be.

As though her thoughts summoned him, he came walking around the side of the inn. He held the phone to his ear. "I'll talk to her. I'm sure it won't be a problem. You have a good time and don't worry about things." There was a slight pause before he said, "Okay. Bye."

Sara couldn't help but wonder if the *her* he'd mentioned was herself. She should keep walking before he glanced up and noticed her, but it was too late. Kent's gaze met hers. She was unable to read his expression. It was as though there was some sort of wall up between them.

To her surprise, he walked right past her. He climbed into his golf cart before driving off without a word to her. Her back teeth ground together. What was it about that man that got to her? He didn't even have to open his mouth to get under her skin.

She set off into town. She walked most everywhere on the island. Bluestar had strict limitations on the use of automobiles. So the residents got around by golf cart, bicycle, or walking. Sara had a bicycle, but she seldom used it.

Why was he being so stubborn about the apartment? She had so much pent-up frustration that it quickened her pace. She didn't have a destination in mind. She just kept walking until she calmed down.

"Hello, Sara."

She immediately recognized the voice. She stopped and turned to find Birdie Neill and her little dog, Peaches. Birdie was a widow and one of the island elders. And was the friendliest person you'd ever want to meet.

Sara smiled. "Hi." When Birdie stopped in front of her, Sara knelt down and fussed over Peaches. "You're so cute." When she straightened, she said, "Are you out for a stroll?"

"We are." Birdie studied her for a moment. "I saw you a little while ago with Kent. You two make such a cute couple."

Heat rushed to Sara's cheeks. "We're not a couple."

"Oh. Pardon me. I just saw you two in the golf cart, and you looked so good together."

Sara shook her head, pushing away the idea of them being a couple. There was absolutely no way she'd ever date such a stubborn man. Even if she were to get past that flaw, there was no way she could get past the fact that he'd broken her sister's heart.

She was always amazed at the way Birdie was able to read people, but in this particular case, Birdie couldn't have been more wrong. She'd become good friends with Birdie once she moved into the second-floor apartment next door to Birdie's house. Her landlord had split their house in half by living in the downstairs and converting the upstairs into a one-bedroom apartment. With it being beachside, it had a million-dollar view. The drawback was the flight of stairs to reach her front door.

Birdie continued to look expectantly at her. She could continue to brush off Birdie's concern, or she could just tell her. She had no doubt that soon it would be town gossip that she was looking for a new place to live. She just hoped her landlord was the last to hear, or she'd have a lot of explaining to do.

"I was just asking him about whether he had any apartments for rent." She felt awkward talking about Kent. When Birdie kept looking at her and not saying anything, Sara rushed on. "You know, over the furniture store."

"Oh yes. And did he?"

"None that he was willing to rent to me."

"That's too bad. There's not much housing available at this time of the year. But you might want to check with Madison St. Claire. I'm sure she's on top of all the available places."

Sara hoped that was the case, since Madison was a real estate agent. "I think I'll stop by her office on my way home."

Birdie frowned. "I'll miss you so much. I really enjoy having you next door. So does Peaches."

"You don't have to worry. It's not for me." She hadn't meant to say that much, but she couldn't let Birdie needlessly worry. "It's for Cari. She's moving back to the island." A smile pulled at the corners of Sara's lips. "I can't wait. She's been gone so long."

"Oh. That's wonderful news. When does she get here?"

"I don't know the details yet, but I'll let you know when I do. I should be going. I want to catch Madison before she goes home."

Birdie nodded in understanding. "I hope you find a place for your sister."

"Thanks. I do too." Her thoughts trailed back to Kent. Why did he have to be so stubborn?

He wanted her to forget about the shabby way he'd treated her sister and start over, but he wasn't ready to do the same by renting her the apartment. Perhaps her sister was fortunate not to have him for a landlord. He'd already caused her enough problems.

It was time to put his plan into action.

Later that evening, Kent pulled out his phone as he searched his fridge for something to eat since he'd skipped dinner. He placed a call to his sister. The line rang once, twice, and then three times. He was beginning to think she wasn't going to pick up.

"Hello."

He closed the fridge empty-handed. "I was beginning to think I missed you."

"I was just getting ready for dinner."

"Dinner?" He glanced at the time on his watch. "It's going on nine o'clock."

"In your part of the world. In California, it's only going on six, and I'm not used to the time change so I'm starving. What did you need? Is everything okay with Mom and Dad?"

"Of course." He started to wonder if there was something about their parents he didn't know—maybe something that was holding them back from agreeing to his new venture. "Why would you ask that?"

"No particular reason. You don't call me that often, and I'm away on vacation. So, I thought it might be something important."

He was relieved to hear there was nothing wrong with their parents. He wasn't sure how to segue into this discussion. All of his carefully-thought-out words suddenly fled him. "This is important."

"Okay. I'm listening."

He sat down on the couch. He supposed he should just start at the beginning. "You know how you ordered some new pieces of furniture for in the lobby?"

"Is there a problem with the order? I had my heart set on the couch and settee. And those armchairs coordinated perfectly with the other pieces."

"No. Everything is fine with the order. In fact, they are supposed to be delivered at the end of next week."

"That's a relief. So, if nothing is wrong with the order, what's bothering you?"

"I was wondering if you would mind if I refreshed the lobby."

There was a distinct pause. "What exactly do you mean by refresh?"

"A fresh coat of paint and a new placement of the furniture. That sort of thing. Nothing major." There was another distinct pause on the other end of the phone. "I wouldn't charge you anything but the cost of the supplies."

"And you're going to do all of this?" There was a note of disbelief in her voice.

"Yes."

"Uh-huh." She didn't sound like she believed he could do it.

"Why are you so skeptical of my abilities?"

"I don't know. It could be the time you convinced me that if you shot your bottle rocket out of my bedroom window that it would go higher and then the bottle ended up falling over and shooting the rocket into my room."

That had been a big miscalculation. One his parents made sure he paid for by being grounded for two weeks and having to do the dishes. "How was I supposed to know that a big gust of wind was going to blow through your window just at the moment I was shooting off the rocket?"

"And then there was the time when you wanted to jerry-rig the riding mower with plywood to make it into some sort of snowplow so you didn't have to shovel the walks."

"Hey, it was a good idea in theory." Two could play this game. "And I remember the time you decided to turn the driveway into your very own ice-skating rink without telling anyone, and Dad totally wiped out on it."

"At least I didn't get the riding mower stuck in a snow drift. Dad was so mad."

They could keep one-upping each other all night. "Okay. Enough. We could do this for hours, and it's getting us nowhere."

"True enough. But you have to realize that the inn is not only my business now, but it's also Lane's."

Kent felt as though his family didn't believe he'd grown up and could make responsible decisions. "If you don't want me to do it, all you have to do is say so. You don't have to throw all of my childhood mistakes in my face."

"I'm sorry. That's not what I was doing. I was just having some fun with you, like we used to do." The regret rang out in her voice. "Kent, what's the matter?"

He told his sister about his idea for the refresh service and how their parents had turned him down. He also told her that he was thinking of quitting the family business and going out on his own.

"Would you really walk away?" she asked.

He shrugged. "I don't know. It's just that I don't feel there's any room for me to grow there—to make some part of the business my own. I spend all day in the office, and I don't mind doing the financial stuff. I actually get some use out of my accounting degree. But lately I'm finding I want to do more than the paperwork."

"And you think this refresh project is what you want to do?"

He honestly didn't know how to answer her. "I won't know until I give it a try."

"What exactly do you have in mind?"

And so he laid out his idea about new paint on the walls. They discussed what color she would like and if it would tie in with the new furniture. He also told her he would reconfigure the furniture, seeing as there were more pieces and different sizes than was originally there.

She also asked that he replace the runner that led from the front door to the registration desk. He didn't see how that would be a problem. He would, however, have to order it, and he couldn't promise that he'd have it by the time she returned to the island in two weeks' time. She assured him that would be fine as long as the other things were complete.

"And you promise you won't make a mess? I have the Carrington wedding in two weeks. It's a big affair, and the inn has to be perfect for it."

"I promise."

There was a slight pause, as though she were rolling the idea around in her mind. "Let me speak to Lane because he's my business partner now. I'll get back to you."

He was suddenly reminded of how his parents kept putting him off, and when he pushed the subject, they'd turned him down. It was a gentle letdown, but it was still a solid *no*.

He didn't want to wait around for another rejection. "You know we're on a timetable with my vacation and the wedding?"

"I understand."

They said their goodbyes, and then Kent was left to wonder what would be decided. He wished he'd had this idea earlier while his sister was still on the island. It would have been much easier to make the pitch in person instead of over the phone.

Maybe his problem was that he'd stayed on this island for too long. Maybe he should be like his older brother, who was now a doctor and lived on the mainland. There would be more opportunities there.

It wasn't the first time he'd had the idea. In fact, he'd had it many times over the years. He'd just never been this restless.

The problem started when his brother Grant declared that he wanted to become a doctor. Their parents looked at Kent as the heir to the furniture store. There was never any real conversation about it—at least none that he could recall.

He opened the fridge again and pulled out some leftover pizza from the other night. In the time it took for him to heat it up in the oven, his phone buzzed. He checked it and found a message from Josie. He'd been given the go ahead to refresh the lobby. He wondered how Sara would feel about having him at the inn.

Chapter Four

His plan was taking shape.

Saturday morning, Kent finished ordering supplies at the hardware store and set off for the inn. He didn't care that it was the weekend. He didn't have time to waste. He wanted everything completed before his sister returned.

He'd spoken to Josie again late last night to go over some details about the refresh. She'd sounded happy. Very happy.

He'd had his reservations about Lane Johnson when he'd shown up on the island, anxious to sell the inn—the inn where his sister had devoted so much of her life. And yet the more he got to know Lane, the more he liked him.

The only thing he couldn't figure out was how his sister and Lane were supposed to make a long-distance relationship work. While Josie lived on the east coast, Lane had his home and business in San Diego. It didn't matter how strong a relationship was; Kent didn't see the relationship going the distance with that sort of mileage between them.

But he couldn't judge their relationship when he was an utter failure when it came to his own relationships.

It wasn't that he didn't date. He did. But he'd learned to do most of his socializing on the mainland. This island was too small to start anything casual on it. As soon as he was spotted with someone, the rumors started about him being in love—even if nothing could be further from the truth. He'd never been in love with anyone—at least he'd never felt anything with the depth that he heard other people talk about.

Now that Sara had pushed her way into his cart yesterday, the rumors were already swirling around the island. Even the guy at the hardware store had heard that he and Sara were an item. And now people wanted to know how Sara's sister felt about the relationship, since he used to date Cari. If only people knew the truth—he wasn't interested in Sara, and he'd never truly dated her sister. It was all an illusion. But that wasn't his story to tell.

He'd been in a rush that morning and headed out the door without breakfast, much less a cup of coffee, and so he stopped at The Lighthouse Café. They had some of the best food and coffee on the island. The place was packed with a mix of tourists and locals. There wasn't a table to be had anywhere.

He headed straight to the long counter at the back of the restaurant. They had four servers on that day. He knew two of them: Lucy and Molly. There was a guy he didn't recognize and another young woman. Two of them were putting in orders with the kitchen. One was carrying a tray of food. And then Lucy rushed over to the cash register. Her long dark ponytail swished back and forth as she rushed around. She had some cash and a slip of paper in her hand.

From beneath her bangs, her gaze lifted to meet his. A smile lit up her face. "Hey, Kent. It's good to see you."

"Thanks. Could I trouble you for a cup of coffee? To go?"

"Sure. Just give me a moment." She rang up the order before slipping the change into her pocket. A couple minutes later, she returned and filled him a to-go cup of steaming coffee. She placed it on the counter in front of him. "Can I get you anything else?"

He eyed up the glazed donut on the counter beneath a glass dome. "Let me have a donut too."

"Certainly. Would you like a second one? Maybe for someone special."

He inwardly groaned. "Not you too."

She smiled and shrugged. "You should know that there aren't any secrets on Bluestar. You riding around town with Sara has been the talk of the town since yesterday. Some already have you two married off."

He sighed. "Some people have really wild imaginations."

"So there's nothing going on between you and Sara?"

He hated discussing his private life, but he knew if he avoided answering her question, it would just escalate the rumors. "No. Nothing at all."

"Interesting. I'll be sure to spread the word."

"Please do."

He picked up his coffee and donut, bid her a good day, and headed out the door. He noticed how heads turned in his direction. Some of the people abruptly stopped talking. He ignored them and kept going out the door.

He turned his thoughts to his plans for the day. He climbed into his golf cart and headed toward the inn. He was eager to get started on this project.

Working with numbers was fine, but sometimes he needed more. He needed to get out of the office and out of the showroom once in a while. He was certain if he could show his parents an actual refresh project, they would agree with his plan.

His first project was to give the lobby of the Brass Anchor Inn a refresh in thirteen days' time. It was plenty of time. He didn't see how a fresh coat of paint and repositioning the new pieces of furniture would take much time. This was going to be so easy.

However, there was a slight delay with the paint. They didn't have it in stock at the store, but they'd have it delivered on Monday. So today he'd take the time to move the furniture away from the walls and cover them with the tarps that he'd just purchased.

He pulled his cart to a stop in the parking lot. He was lucky to find an available spot. It appeared the inn was booked. He wasn't surprised. Bluestar Island was a popular vacation spot.

With it being the weekend, he didn't know if Sara would be at the inn. A part of him hoped to avoid her, but the other part wanted to explain his presence at the inn, and hopefully, it would be the end of their interactions. She could go back to her work while he made the updates to the lobby. He knew she didn't want to spend any further time with him than he did with her.

He made his way up the walk before crossing the wide porch that was lined with white rocking chairs and potted flowers in shades of pink and yellow. He pulled open the front door. It took his eyes a moment to adjust to the dim lighting after the bright sunshine.

There was no one in the lobby. It gave him a chance to look around. Now that he was looking at the room with an eye to decorating, he noticed it was larger than he'd recalled.

He moved slowly around the room, taking in all the memorabilia. His footsteps were muffled by the thick navy-blue carpeting. This room was filled with so much of Bluestar's history. The previous owner had worked hard to collect the various pieces of the island's history. He'd be the first to admit that she'd been quite successful. She'd assembled it all here as a sort of museum.

The blue painted walls were lined with black-and-white photos of Bluestar Island throughout the years. As he looked at each individual photo, he felt as though he were walking back through time. They definitely needed to keep this important element in the room. He just wondered if there was a better way to display things.

He moved to the wall and removed one of the framed photos. He looked at the back of the frame and found that it had a wire across the back that attached to the hook on the wall.

"Put it back!"

The familiar voice came from behind him. He turned around and met Sara's narrowed gaze. "I can explain."

She took a few more steps toward him but left a respectable distance between them. She frowned at him as she took the photograph from him. "Didn't you read the sign that says no touching?"

"I was just checking it out for the refresh."

Her brows drew together. "The what?"

"Didn't you talk to my sister?"

"Of course I talk to her. She's my boss." Sara moved past him and proceeded to hang the picture on the wall once more.

When she turned around, he said, "I meant did you talk to her today?"

She checked her fitness watch. "Not hardly. It's not even six a.m. on the west coast. *And* it's the weekend."

"Why are you working on a Saturday?"

"I'm not—officially that is. I just stopped in to check on things."

He nodded in understanding. He did the same thing at the furniture store. "When you talk to Josie, she'll tell you that I'm going to be doing a bit of redecorating."

"Decorating?" Her forehead creased with lines. "Where?"

"Here." Obviously, this was going to take more explanation than he'd been anticipating.

— *ele* —

He couldn't be serious.

Sara stood in front of Kent. Her gaze held his. There was no smile on his face. And there was no amusement in his eyes.

He was serious. He intended to redecorate the inn's lobby.

She pursed her lips and frowned at him. "You can't."

"Actually, I can."

"I mean the inn is booked. To mess up the lobby now would create unnecessary havoc."

He nodded as though he understood her problem with his plan. "I talked about that with Josie. It was her concern too. We decided there was no good time to do this, and seeing as the new furniture she ordered is due to be delivered by the end of next week, she gave me the go ahead."

"But there's a huge wedding in thirteen day. I can't have the inn all messed up. There will be photos and guests. Lots of guests. They rented out the entire inn for that weekend."

"I guess this means I better get to work."

Sara crossed her arms as she continued to frown at him. "Can't you move this to another time? Like next month? Or maybe after the summer rush?"

He shook his head. "I'm afraid not. I need to have this place ready for the furniture delivery."

Sara opened her mouth to further argue the point, but if Josie, who now owned half of the inn, had approved this plan, she had no choice but to go along with it. The only thing she could do was make sure he completed this refresh as quickly as possible.

It was her chance to prove to Josie and Lane that she was capable of taking on greater responsibility. And now her chance of doing that was resting on Kent pulling off this redecorating thing in a timely manner. She didn't like relying on other people. It never worked out for her.

She drew in a deep breath and released it. "How do you intend to do this without interrupting business?"

He paused as though he hadn't given it any thought. He glanced around the room as though trying to come up with a plan. "I guess we could section off part of the lobby."

She surveyed the room. The registration desk was on one side, and on the other side was seating and Bluestar memorabilia. There was no way you could only decorate part of the room. Whatever was done to one part had to be done to the other part.

She wondered just how many times Kent had redecorated. She thought of asking him, but bit back the words. Instead she asked, "So you're only fixing up part of the room?"

"No. Of course not."

"Then your idea won't work."

He frowned at her. "What would you suggest?"

Of course he'd leave it up to her. She withheld a sigh. "I don't know. This is the first I'm hearing of it."

"I apologize for springing this on you. The thing is I promised my sister the work would be completed by the time she returned. That doesn't leave me much time."

Wait. Had he just apologized to her? Maybe he wasn't so bad after all. Or maybe he was just saying whatever he could to gain her help?

She moved toward the wide hallway leading to the dining room and other community rooms. There were double doors that led out into the garden. It was really the only reasonable solution.

"This will have to be the temporary check-in area."

Kent turned around in a circle as though evaluating the area. "Works for me."

"Now we need a temporary reception desk and signs."

"Don't worry about all of that. I'll take care of it."

She arched a brow. "Are you sure?"

He nodded before he set off. She watched him go. She couldn't believe she'd have to put up with him for the next twelve days. Hopefully, they could avoid each other as much as possible.

CHAPTER FIVE

IT WAS GETTING LATE.

Sunday afternoon, Kent couldn't believe how long it was taking him to empty the lobby. The room held so much more stuff than he'd ever imagined. There were dozens and dozens of framed photos on the walls. And there were display cases with so much stuff in them. Each display had to be taken apart before it could be moved.

Even worse, once he moved things around, it was obvious the carpeting was worn out. He sighed. This job was getting more complicated by the minute.

And then there was Sara. She didn't say anything to him, but from time to time she would step up to the doorway, cross her arms, and frown at him. She was the one person on this island who he didn't get along with. He didn't think that would ever change.

He was surprised to see her working all weekend. He had a feeling she was picking up extra shifts because his sister/her boss was out of town.

"How's it going?" Sara took a step into the room.

He rested against a display case that he had been slowly moving across the room. "It's going."

Her gaze surveyed the room. "You're going to put everything back where you found it, aren't you?"

"That's going to be difficult."

She arched a brow. "Why?"

"Because Josie ordered new furniture that isn't the same size or the same quantity as the current pieces."

Sara stared down at the carpet. "It won't work. The carpet is a wreck."

She was right. He had a feeling his sister didn't have any clue how worn the carpet was, or she would have insisted on replacing it too.

"I don't know what to tell you." He stared at the carpet, noticing the worn marks from people walking in between the display cases and the stains that had been covered by the furniture.

"Put the old furniture back. We have the Carrington wedding coming up. We can't have the lobby looking like this."

He rubbed the back of his neck as he tried to come up with a remedy that didn't involve replacing the carpeting. "Maybe we could put down some throw rugs."

Sara frowned at him. "We need the furniture back." She looked around. "Where is it?"

"Gone."

She gaped at him. "What do you mean gone?"

"I gave the pieces away. Some kids came and took them."

"Well, call them. Tell them you need them back."

He shook his head. "I can't."

"Yes, you can."

"No, seriously I can't. I don't have any way to reach them."

Her mouth opened, but no words came out. She pressed her lips together. They formed a distinct frown.

He didn't like that she frowned at him so much. He'd much prefer one of her sunny smiles that she shared so freely with others. She'd never liked him. She always held the breakup with her sister against him.

He couldn't help but wonder if she would feel differently about him if she knew the truth. He was so tempted to tell her, but it wasn't his truth to tell. And so he remained silent.

"What are we going to do about this?" Sara looked expectantly at him.

He knew what the answer was going to be, but he didn't want to admit it to her or even himself. Replacing the carpeting was going to be far more involved than a fresh coat of paint and the new configuration of the furniture.

"What do you think we should do?" he countered.

"We? This is your problem. Not mine."

"Yes, but you're the one with the pressing timeline. So, you might have to help out."

She shook her head as she waved off the idea. "I can't. I have a job to do."

He looked pointedly at her. "If you want this done quickly, I'm going to need some help."

"I don't understand how the problem you created has suddenly become my problem too."

He met her steady gaze and held it. "Are you going to help? Or not?"

She was quiet for a moment. The look in her eyes let him know that she was rolling around her options. He was almost afraid to hear what she would say. He sensed she was up to something.

She arched a brow. "I'll help you on one condition."

He knew it was going to cost him. "What's that?"

"I want the apartment."

He'd thought she'd given up on the apartment. The thought of dealing with her on a daily basis was just too much. He wasn't willing to do it.

"I don't think so." He'd find someone else to help him. Maybe one of his brothers would lend a hand.

She shrugged her shoulders. "Suit yourself. Just make sure this area looks perfect in time for the wedding."

She turned and walked away. He couldn't help but watch her make an exit. He felt as though he'd dodged a bullet. Working with her wouldn't have been fun. That was for sure—not with the way she was always frowning at him.

This week was not going to be fun.

Monday morning, Sara was up extra early. She'd had a restless night. She rushed to her galley kitchen. She was grateful it only took a couple of minutes for her coffeemaker to heat up. In no time, her to-go cup was filled with hot coffee.

Already dressed as well as having her hair and makeup done, she grabbed her purse and headed for the door.

As she pulled the door shut behind her, her thoughts returned to Kent. She didn't know why she let him get to her. It had to stop. She would treat him just like any other employee or in this case a contractor that had been hired to do work on the inn.

She told herself it was the fact that Kent had wrecked the lobby that bothered her. It had absolutely nothing to do with his sexy good looks or the way his dark brows drew together when he was deep in thought or how his sky-blue eyes felt as though they could see through her. *Nope.* It couldn't be any of those because he was Cari's ex. He had broken her sister's heart. Sisters didn't date each other's ex. It just wasn't done. Not that she was thinking of dating him.

It was easier to be angry with him than to accept that she found him distractingly handsome. And so she centered her thoughts on the problem at the moment: the carpeting. Shouldn't he have expected the carpeting to be damaged? Isn't that his job to anticipate those sorts of things?

It seemed like he was destined to create trouble for her. First, with her sister and now with her job—a job she enjoyed very much. She had to stop him from making things worse.

As she made her way down the steps from her second-floor apartment, she heard a familiar voice call out her name. She glanced at the house next door and found Birdie sitting on her porch with her dog, Peaches. "Good morning."

"It's going to be a beautiful day." Birdie studied her. "What's wrong?"

"Why would you ask that?"

"Because you were frowning, and the day has barely even started. What's worrying you?"

She was frowning? She hadn't realized her thoughts had translated onto her face. She'd have to work better at concealing her thoughts if she ever wanted to be an effective manager.

Since she'd moved next door to Birdie, the woman had become a surrogate grandmother to her. Birdie was easy to talk to and she kept Sara's confidence. Although in this particular situation, she didn't see how Birdie would be able to offer any words of advice. Still, it would help to get it all off her chest.

And so, Sara told Birdie about the situation at the inn with Kent giving away the original furniture without even considering the problem with the carpeting. "Now I don't know if he'll have the room completed in time for this big wedding we're hosting. And I promised Josie that I could handle everything while she was gone. I don't want to let her down."

"You won't." There was a note of confidence in Birdie's voice.

"I hope you're right. This project just seems to keep growing."

"I see." Birdie paused as though to give it some thought. "Why don't you help him?"

Immediately, Sara shook her head. "I don't think it's a good idea."

"Why not?"

"Well, first because I already have a job running the inn."

"Of course. But what's the other reason?"

"Other reason?"

Birdie nodded. "You said first because you have your day job, and that would lead to a second reason. What is it?"

Sara had been hoping to avoid this part. "You know that he used to date my sister?" When Birdie nodded, she said, "Well, I feel like I'm betraying my sister by partnering up with him."

"But that was so long ago. I'm sure Cari has forgotten all about it. And it's not like you're going out on a date with him. This would be strictly work."

When Birdie said it, she made it sound so simple and straightforward. But when Sara was around Kent, nothing felt simple. He made her heart race, and she struggled to maintain her line of thought. No one ever rattled her the way he did, and she didn't like feeling off kilter around him.

"I don't think it's a good idea."

"But you do want the lobby finished in time for the wedding, don't you?"

Sara glanced at the time on her fitness watch. "I'll give it some thought on my way to the inn." She got to her feet and pet Peaches. "You are so sweet."

"You should consider getting a pet. I just love having Peaches. I'd be lost without her."

"I don't know. I work a lot. I don't know if it would be fair to a dog to be closed in much of the day."

"Just a thought."

Sara bent over to give Peaches one last pet before straightening. "I have to get to the inn. I hope you have a nice day."

"You've already made it a lovely day. There's nothing better than spending a little porch time with a dear friend."

Birdie's words touched Sara's heart. As she walked away, she waved at some other Bluestar residents who were out for a morning walk. This island was filled with some of the nicest people. She couldn't imagine ever moving away.

Her phone vibrated. She lifted it up to find a message from the night manager, letting her know about a problem with one of the guest rooms. She'd asked him to keep her updated on any problems at the inn. She texted back, thanking him for the update and let him know that she'd be there shortly.

And then she noticed there was a voicemail. She listened to it and found it was a message from her sister. Sara was disappointed that she'd missed Cari's call. The message was short and ended with her sister asking if she had found her an available apartment on the island.

Sara had spoken with Madison, the island's real estate agent, over the weekend. Madison told her she didn't know of any available units. She also mentioned a rumor about an apartment becoming available at the end of the month, but she wouldn't divulge any of the details.

Sara knew Madison was referring to the apartment above the furniture store. It appeared there would be great demand for it. If she didn't do something soon, it would be gone.

Sara's thoughts turned to Kent and his refusal to rent her the apartment. She wondered if he'd found someone to help him with the lobby. If not, perhaps he would be in the mood to negotiate. She hoped so. Her footsteps picked up as she headed to the inn.

Chapter Six

"**C**OME ON. SURELY YOU have some time to help me."

Kent stood outside of the inn, holding his phone to his ear. He continued to pace back and forth on the wide, sweeping porch. He'd already called his younger brother Jack, whom he woke up. Jack hadn't been happy about the earliness of the hour. Wasn't everyone awake by seven thirty? Apparently not in his younger brother's case.

Then he'd called Owen, who was thankfully awake. But trying to persuade him to help with the flooring at the inn wasn't going well.

"I can't help you out," Owen said. "I've got my own problems."

"What problems could you have? You play video games all day?"

There was a distinct silence. "I write programs for video games. There's a difference."

Kent stopped pacing and raked his fingers through his hair. "I'm sorry. I know there is, and I know you're really good at what you do, but I've really messed up. I just need some help with getting the flooring in as soon as possible or Josie is going to flip out."

"I wish I could help you, but I have my own deadline at the end of the week. Why don't you call Jack?"

"I already did. All I got was a bunch of grunts, and then he hung up."

"I don't know what to tell you. There has to be someone on the island that has time to help you. Ask around. I've got to run. I'll talk to you later."

The line went dead.

Kent wanted to throw in the towel on his refresh idea. His parents were against it. And his first project wasn't going well. But he was too far into the project to back out now. The lobby couldn't be left as it was.

He'd talked to his sister the night before. After hearing about the problem, she was ready to fly home and oversee everything, but between him and Lane, they were able to assure her that Kent would take care of everything.

Once his sister had calmed down, they'd talked over what sort of flooring would be appropriate for the lobby. She'd told him she wanted to move away from the carpeting. It was just too hard to maintain with the sand and in the winter the snow. She would prefer some sort of tile in a lighter shade.

He'd gone to the flooring store in town and was relieved to find that they had a gray vinyl tile with wood grain in it. He sent a photo to his sister, who gave it a thumbs up. While the store didn't have enough stock on hand, they had enough for him to get started and promised the rest in a day or two.

It would give him time to pull up the old carpeting. After which he was going to prime the walls. It was going to be a busy day and without any help, it was going to be an extremely long day as well. Even with him working round the clock, he wasn't sure he would get it done in time for the wedding.

He was still on the porch when Sara approached him. He couldn't make out what she was thinking because her very expressive eyes were hidden behind a dark pair of sunglasses.

She had on a white blouse with a blue vest over it and a gold nametag. A royal blue skirt stopped a few inches above her knees. And on her feet were tennis shoes for walking to work. He had no doubt she'd eventually switch into heels.

She looked good—really good. It wasn't until he lifted his gaze that he realized he'd been caught checking her out. Suddenly, it became quite warm outside.

He swallowed hard. "Good morning."

She came to a stop in front of him. "Were you able to find someone to help you with the flooring?"

Of course she would start with the one subject he didn't want to discuss. "No. I haven't."

"And will you be able to finish the project in time for the upcoming wedding?"

He hesitated. He wasn't used to being put in the position of failure. He always excelled at whatever he did from academics to sports. And so he wasn't going to fail at this either. "One way or the other."

"What if I help you?"

Surely he hadn't heard her correctly. He once more took in her blouse and skirt. They definitely weren't the sort of clothes to paint in or to lay some flooring.

Still he was curious. "What do you mean by help?"

She sent him a little smile. "I didn't know it was that hard to understand. I mean I'll help you with the flooring." She glanced around. "And whatever else you need."

She was up to something, but he wasn't sure about her end game. "Have you ever laid flooring?"

"No. But how hard can it be?"

He'd had the same thought when he'd taken on this project. He was quickly finding out that some things that seemed simple enough were anything but.

He shook his head. "I don't think so."

She pressed her hands to her slightly rounded hips. "May I ask why not?"

His mind raced. He decided to throw her earlier excuse back in her face. "Because you have the inn to run."

"I can do both."

He arched a disbelieving brow. Again he said, "I don't think so."

"Well, since I'm in charge of the inn while your sister is away, I'm the boss, and I'm telling you that I'm helping."

He was impressed with her take-charge mode. Maybe it wouldn't be so bad having her help. He could find her some easy jobs to do. "Fine. You can help."

"Not so fast."

Her words drew him up short. The little hairs on the back of his neck stood up. He had a feeling that this had been some sort of trap, and he'd unknowingly fallen straight into it.

He shifted his weight from one foot to the other. "What's the problem?"

"My help is going to cost you. I want you to rent me the apartment."

He sighed. "What is it with you and that apartment? You already have a much better apartment."

"How do you know?"

He might have asked someone where she lived because he was curious about why she'd want to move—that was the only reason. "Everyone knows where you live. It's a small island. So what gives? Is the apartment really for you?"

She was quiet for a moment, as though trying to decide how best to answer his question. "No, it's not."

"Who's it for?"

"Does it matter?"

He nodded. "If I'm going to have someone in my building, yes, it matters."

Her gaze lowered to the floor before rising once more to meet his. "It's for my sister."

"Cari?" He had no idea she was moving back to the island.

"Of course. How many sisters do you think I have?"

"It's just that I thought she was in Japan or China or something."

"She's in Malaysia. And she wants to come home, but she's having a really hard time finding someplace to live.

I'd let her stay with me, but I have a small one-bedroom apartment. There just isn't room."

He didn't like the thought of having Cari in his family's building. At one point they'd been good friends—good enough that he'd agreed to be her fake boyfriend for the summer. It had been a huge mistake, but by the time he'd figured that out, it was too late.

He raked his fingers through his hair. "It's not a good idea."

"You mean because you two used to date?"

He nodded. He couldn't believe that Cari never told her sister the truth about them, especially when Sara was her ardent defender. Sara hadn't cared who heard her when she'd told him off for dumping her sister. It had been the most embarrassing moment of his life.

The tip of Sara's tongue wet her lips. "It was Cari's idea. I think she's desperate."

Was it possible they could finally put the past behind them? The idea appealed to him. This was a very small island, and it was difficult to avoid people—people like Sara and her sister.

"And you think this is a good idea?" His gaze searched Sara's face for the truth and not just what she wanted him to hear.

"I think what happened was pretty crummy, but it was a long time ago. If you can be man enough to rent Cari the apartment, I think we can put the whole affair behind us."

She'd said exactly what he wanted to hear, but did she believe her own words? Or had she said them purely to get him to agree to rent Cari the apartment? There was no way to know. He could either give her the benefit of the doubt or continue this pettiness into the future. The latter part did not appeal to him. The truth was that he used to like Sara. She could be friendly and easy-going. The idea of being her friend definitely appealed to him.

It was on the tip of his tongue to agree to this idea, but then he had a thought. "Are you sure Cari is going to be okay with this plan?"

"She doesn't have to know about the plan. All she's concerned about is having a place to live. But if you're worried there will be some sort of awkwardness every time you see each other, I wouldn't be. It was her idea to rent your apartment."

He couldn't ask for any more than that. He held his hand out to her. When she placed her hand in his, he wasn't prepared for the electrical jolt that traveled up his arm and set his heart pounding. He was going to say something, but in that moment, the words fled him.

"It's a deal, isn't it?" She sent him a puzzled look.

"It is."

She withdrew her hand, and he immediately missed her touch. "I won't be able to help you this morning, but I'll speak to Harvey and see if he can start a little early so I can help you this afternoon and into the evening. Will that work?"

He nodded. "I'll see you later." He started for the door and then turned back. "I hope you have some work clothes to change into. I'd hate to see you mess up that pretty outfit." And then feeling daring, maybe because of the way his heart was still tap-dancing in his chest, he said, "It looks really good on you."

Pink stained her cheeks, but she smiled. It was one of those smiles that lit up her entire face. At last, he was the recipient of her glorious smiles. His work was done here.

Realizing he'd said more than enough, he opened the door and proceeded to enter the lobby. It wasn't until he was inside with the door shut that he stopped and wondered what in the world had gotten into him.

It was all going to work out.

Sara kept telling herself that throughout the day. She'd spoken to Harvey about coming in a little early to give her time to work on the lobby refresh, and he'd agreed. It was a good start.

Although, she knew there were so many unknowns with the deal she'd struck with Kent. Even with her help, would they complete the lobby in time for the wedding? She hoped so. It was the only way she could prove to Josie she was capable of greater responsibility.

So that morning, she'd worked nonstop on the daily reports and the mail. She'd checked in with the staff, making sure that everything was running smoothly. And finally at lunchtime, she'd rushed home to pick up some shorts and a T-shirt.

When three o'clock rolled around, Harvey showed up at the inn as agreed. He looked a bit dressed up for work, and Sara became suspicious.

"Hi, Harvey. Thanks so much for agreeing to help out." As she took in his pressed shirt with a yellow carnation in his pocket right above his gold nametag, she just had to ask, "Is there something special going on today?"

"What?" He sent her a confused look. When she gestured to the flower, he yanked it out of his pocket. "I had a lunch date. It was a blind date with someone visiting the island. The flower was so she would recognize me."

Harvey was a widower, and Sara was so happy to see him getting on with his life. "That's great! I hope it went well."

He shook his head. "It didn't. The woman was too busy telling me about her favorite soap opera for us to have any sort of meaningful conversation."

"I'm so sorry, but the right woman is out there. You just have to keep looking." But she noticed he looked a bit off. Maybe he was tired, and then she felt guilty for asking him to take on some of her work. "Hey, Harvey, if coming in early is too much, I can figure out something else."

He once more shook his head. "It's not a problem. With Melinda being so busy with her bookshop and stuff, I like to keep busy. So, I don't mind at all."

Melinda was his daughter and Sara's good friend who owned the Seaside Bookshop. Sara had known Melinda most of her life. They'd helped each other through the good times and the bad—as they'd both lost their mothers.

Sara smiled. "Thank you so much. If you need anything, just come get me."

"I will, but this appears to be a quiet afternoon."

"It is. Thanks again." And then she was off.

She changed clothes and headed to the lobby. She was surprised by the progress Kent had made. He had the old carpeting rolled up. The remaining furniture had been moved to one side of the room.

"Wow. You got a lot done."

Kent straightened and looked around. "This project has certainly grown from what I initially thought I'd be doing."

"And it's going to look great when it's completed."

His eyes widened. "Do you really think so?"

"I do. Why do you look so surprised?"

"Because you were so against this project."

"It... It wasn't the project." She paused as though to gather her thoughts. "It was the timing of everything. But I guess there would never be a good time. Now where do you want me?"

He'd given it a lot of thought, and he had a plan in mind. "How are you at painting?"

"Painting?" Surprise rang out in her voice. "I thought we were laying flooring."

"We will, but I think we should prime the walls and get them painted first so there's no chance of messing up the new floor."

She sent him a smile and nodded. "Good thinking."

"I picked up the primer this morning. It's over in the corner." He led the way.

He could get used to this friendly side of Sara. Perhaps by the end of this project, they might have something that loosely resembled a friendship. Stranger things had happened on the island.

CHAPTER SEVEN

WHO KNEW PAINTING WAS so much work? Sara's arms were sore. She'd used muscles she hadn't even known she had. She'd climbed a ladder, only to still have to reach as high as she could to reach the ceiling, and then she had to crouch down to paint the wall near the floor. She was constantly in motion. This lobby was so much larger than she'd thought.

Of course, it took her longer to do her parts because she'd been elected to use a brush to paint along the molding and the corners because it took a steady hand. It also took all of her concentration as she painted from top to bottom.

Kent followed her with a paint roller to cover the main expanse of the wall. He worked the roller in a W-pattern across the wall. As they worked together, the room slowly transformed before their eyes.

Sara bent over and stretched out her muscles. She was going to have to start going back to yoga at Beach Love Yoga. She'd stopped in order to... She couldn't remember why she'd stopped. But it was definitely time to get back to it.

"Thank you for your help," Kent said. "You're good with a paint brush."

"Thanks. I've had some experience. I painted my childhood home before it was sold." The thought filled her with sadness. She'd never wanted to part with the house, but it was just too much for her to keep up with on her own. "And then I painted my entire apartment before I moved in. It made it feel more like my own place."

"So what you're saying is that you're secretly a professional painter."

She let out a laugh. "I definitely wouldn't go that far, but I do okay with a paint roller in my hand."

"Good. Because we have to paint over this primer tomorrow."

"Oh, lucky us." She leaned her upper body to one side, straightened, and then leaned to the other side. When she straightened again, she asked, "What's next?"

His brows rose. "You want more work to do tonight?"

She shrugged. Her muscles groaned with every movement. Her stomach protested the fact they'd skipped dinner. She hoped Kent hadn't heard the noise.

Not willing to give in to her body's demands, she said, "I'm willing to do whatever it takes to finish this project."

"Well, we can't do it all in one night. And we can't have you making yourself sick from malnourishment." He closed the primer can and wiped off his hands. "I say we grab some dinner."

She had no idea what time it was because she'd taken off her fitness watch when she'd started painting to keep it from getting splattered. She retrieved it from her pocket and was surprised to find it was going on eight o'clock.

"I guess you're right. I had no idea it was this late."

Together they cleaned up their equipment so that everything would be ready for them tomorrow. They exited the front door, and she made sure to lock it. She repositioned the sign directing guests to the temporary entrance to the inn.

Then she turned to him. "Well...um, goodnight."

He didn't say anything for a moment. "Do you want to grab something to eat?"

She mentally inventoried her fridge at home and realized she'd been so busy over the weekend that she'd failed to pick up any groceries. So if she went directly home, her choices would be a can of soup or ramen noodles. Neither appealed to her. Her stomach growled again as she thought of food.

"I can see by the look on your face that you don't have anything at home you're anxious to eat, so come with me." He waved for her to follow him to his golf cart.

In that moment, she was too tired to argue. The thought of someone else preparing the food and cleaning up the dishes definitely appealed to her.

"Are you sure?" she asked. "I don't want to intrude on your plans for the evening."

He shook his head. "You aren't intruding on anything. With or without you, I still have to grab something to eat. What are you hungry for?"

Her mind filled with ideas from pizza to tacos. It all sounded good to her. She couldn't remember the last time she was this hungry. "I'm not picky."

"How about a burger at the Purple Guppy?"

Her stomach growled its approval. "And onion rings? They make the best."

"Of course."

He was a man after her own stomach. Maybe there were some good qualities to the guy—even if he had devastated her sister.

The ride to the Purple Guppy was quiet. She glanced around, wondering who would see her in Kent's cart and once more start gossiping about them going to dinner together. Not that there was anything to their dinner. It was strictly for business purposes.

Luckily for her, not many people were out and about. Most were probably at home or grabbing a bite to eat.

Every now and then, her gaze would stray to the left and land on Kent. He'd grown even more handsome over the years, and he'd certainly filled out. Then, realizing she was staring, she glanced away.

Her gaze landed on a utility pole. There was a colorful poster on it announcing Bluestar's Concert on the Beach Summer Spectacular. It was the same weekend as the Carrington wedding. Instead of having another two-day event, they'd decided to cut it back to one day. She hadn't decided if she'd be attending or not.

The cart slowed down. With it being later in the evening, there was parking right in front of the restaurant. And they were seated immediately.

She glanced around at the purple, black, and white decor. But it was the large aquariums that caught and held her attention. She loved watching the colorful fish swimming through the elaborately decorated tanks.

"It doesn't matter how many times I come in here," she said, "I always find something new that I hadn't noticed before. Like that orange fish painted on the wall. I swear that wasn't there the last time I was here."

He smiled as he checked out the fish she was pointing to. "Do you always notice things like that?"

She nodded. "I really like their decor. It's fun. And their food is even better."

The server arrived at their table with two glasses of water. "Do you need more time to look at the menu?"

They simultaneously said no. They ended up with the same order: burgers and onion rings.

After the server walked off to place their order, a silence settled over their table. Earlier that day they'd both been so busy painting and working that their conversation was mostly based on their work. But now she wasn't sure what to talk to him about. She honestly didn't know that much about him.

"Do you come here often?" she asked.

He leaned back. "Not that much. I normally order pizza. I like it because there's leftovers for the next day or two."

She picked up a display card in the center of the table. It had a picture of what looked to be a delicious chocolate cake with a scoop of vanilla bean ice cream. "Mm... Maybe we should get this for dessert." She turned the card around for him to see. "We could share it."

Kent shook his head. "I don't like chocolate."

"Are you serious?" She didn't know anyone who didn't like chocolate—well, at least until now.

He nodded. "I know I'm strange."

"Not strange. Just different."

The awkward silence quickly returned. He certainly wasn't a big conversationalist. Maybe she just needed to tackle the elephant in the room. It wasn't like she hadn't wanted to bring up the subject of her sister earlier that day. It just never seemed like the right time.

"So what happened between you and my sister? One minute you guys were spending every weekend together and then nothing." She wanted to say that he'd skipped out on her sister the evening of their cousin's wedding. It had been the talk at the reception. And by morning, the gossip mill in Bluestar had spread it all over town.

He looked at her. His eyes were unreadable. "I wondered how long it'd be until you brought up the subject again."

"And how did I do?"

"Actually, you held out longer than I thought you would."

She noticed he was avoiding answering her question. And she had to ask herself why. It had happened a long time ago. Why hadn't her sister or Kent cleared the air and explained what had happened between them.

"So what's the answer?" She couldn't just let it go now that they were working together.

He sighed. "It's not my truth to give you."

"What's that supposed to mean?"

"It means I'm surprised your sister never told you."

She'd never pressed Cari, because she'd seemed so upset at the time. And then after the rumors quieted, Sara hadn't wanted to bring it up and upset her sister all over again. She'd been curious, but she figured if her sister wanted to talk about it, she would have.

She tucked her hair behind her ear. "Well, she didn't, so I'd like you to tell me your side of things. Why did you break my sister's heart?"

She noticed how his eyes briefly widened as though she'd surprised him with the accusation. Why would he be surprised? There was no way he didn't know how her sister felt. They'd been serious all that summer.

He shook his head. "Sara, I can't talk to you about this."

"Yes, you can. Just tell me what happened."

"I can't." There was no emotion in his firm words.

"Why are you being so stubborn?"

"Because it's not my truth to share."

"What does that mean? Are you saying my sister has a secret?"

He was quiet as he glanced over at the other tables, as though he were wishing he could get far away from her. Finally, he turned his attention back to her. "I'm saying that it was a long time ago. You just need to let it go."

The server showed up with their food. All the while she wondered why Kent was being so secretive. It was obvious he wasn't going to tell her anything. Even though it frustrated her, it also impressed her the way he was willing to keep things private.

She let go of the subject for now and focused on the delicious food. She added some ketchup to her plate and dipped an onion ring in it. She noticed he'd added mustard to his plate and dipped his onion rings in it. To each his own.

She tried to think up something to make small talk about. "So how did you get time away from the furniture store?"

"I had a lot of unused vacation time, so I decided to take some of it."

"And you thought that you'd use the time to redecorate your sister's inn? Wouldn't you rather have been laying on the beach? Or visiting another part of the country?"

He shrugged as he picked up his burger. "The thought crossed my mind."

She took a sip of her ice water. "So, why did you decide to stay and work?"

He took a bite of his burger. After he swallowed, he said, "I'm not doing the lobby out of the goodness of my heart."

"Oh." She had absolutely no idea what his ulterior motive might be, but she was curious.

"For a long time now, I've wanted to expand the furniture store. Sort of put my own stamp on it and make it feel more like my own."

She nodded. "I can understand that. Hasn't the business been in your family for a long time?"

"My great grandfather started it. And it hasn't changed much since those days. I mean it's all automated now, but the basic structure of the business is the same. We sell household furniture."

"And you would like to switch things up a bit?"

"Exactly. I've tried over time to find something new to add to the business, but for one reason or another, my parents always have a reason why it shouldn't be done."

She wouldn't have any idea what that would be like, since her mother died when she was young, and her father pretty much kept to himself until he passed on. She and her sister had to find their own way in life.

"I'm sorry they wouldn't share your vision for the future of the business. But what does that have to do with the inn?"

He took his last onion ring and swiped up the remaining mustard on his plate before popping it into his mouth. Once he swallowed, he wiped off his fingers on his napkin. "You don't want to hear about this."

Totally full, she pushed away her plate with some of her onion rings still on it. "Actually, I am interested, if you're willing to share."

"Well, why don't we get out of here, and I'll tell you?"

She nodded in agreement.

When she reached for her wallet, he said, "It's on me."

She continued to get out some cash. "Maybe another time but tonight we're going Dutch."

Once their bills were paid and a generous tip was left, they headed outside. It was a warm evening with lots of stars in the sky. On such a beautiful evening, she preferred to walk on the beach.

When Kent headed for his cart, she said, "I think I'm going to walk from here."

"Mind if I walk with you?"

She arched a brow. "Are you afraid I'll get lost on the way home?"

"No. If you don't want me to walk with you, all you have to do is say so. But I thought you wanted to hear about why I was working on the lobby."

She nodded. "Let's go." She led the way to the beach. "Sometimes in the evening, I like to walk here. It's so much quieter than during the day when all of the tourists are out and about."

He glanced around at a few other couples walking along the water's edge. "It is peaceful."

Her gaze kept straying to the other couples. One couple stopped to share a kiss. Suddenly, her idea for a moonlit walk didn't seem like such a good idea.

She swallowed hard as she glanced away. "So, why are you working on the lobby?"

"I had this idea to add a service to the business..."

He continued to tell her about his refresh service as they walked along the beach. She found that she enjoyed his company, and the sound of his deep voice was soothing. If he hadn't dated her sister, she could see them exploring this thing between them. After all, she'd had a crush on him before her sister dated him. But that was a long time ago.

Chapter Eight

H ER HEART RACED.

The moonlight cast a romantic glow over them.

Sara struggled not to glance in Kent's direction. She could sense the tension running between them. It wasn't the same awkwardness that had existed when she first approached him about the apartment. This tension was much different.

Her stomach shivered with nerves. And she was aware of just how close he was to her. If she were to lean to the side just a bit, their shoulders would bump. Not that she was going to do such a thing.

Instead, as they walked their hands accidentally brushed each other. She resisted the urge to reach out and slip her hand into his. She didn't know why she'd had the thought. It was so wrong. Sisters didn't move in on the other sister's guys, past or present. It just wasn't something they did.

She inwardly groaned. Why was she thinking of Kent in that way? It wasn't like she was interested in him. She didn't even trust him at this point. He was still holding out about the past. Why wouldn't he tell her?

Sure, he'd said it wasn't his story to tell. Was that the truth or was he hiding something? Well, if it wasn't his story to tell, that meant her sister was keeping a secret from her. The thought didn't sit well with her. She'd always thought they confided in each other. At least she'd always confided in her sister. Surely her sister wouldn't be holding out on her—especially when Cari knew how upset Sara had been with Kent after their break up.

"What has you so quiet?" His voice drew her from her thoughts.

There was no way she was telling him the truth. She wasn't going to let him think she was that hung up on him. Because she wasn't. Sure, she'd had a massive crush on him years ago and had been heartbroken when her sister started to date him, but that was all in the distant past.

"Nothing." And then realizing he would keep pestering her until she gave him a legitimate answer, she said, "I'm just a bit tired. I'm not used to all of that painting." She glanced over at him. "You don't seem tired. You must do a lot of this kind of work."

He shook his head. "I wouldn't say a lot of it. I help out here and there if my family or friends need a hand fixing up their place. I know it'll sound strange, but I find painting relaxing. I enjoy it."

"That's not strange at all. It's great that you've found something you enjoy. Maybe you should do it all of the time."

He shrugged. "I don't know. I guess that's what I'll figure out over these next couple of weeks." He glanced at her.

"What about you? What do you enjoy doing when you're not working at the inn?"

"I like to read."

"Read? What sorts of books?"

"Mostly what the book club picks. Sometimes I'll also read some romances and mysteries. It depends on how much time I have."

"What's this book club you mentioned?"

"There's a group of us that meet over at the Seaside Bookshop. It started with just four of us, but now we're up to eight people. We take turns each month picking out a book."

"So, it's a bunch of women who get together once a week?"

"No. The group actually includes a couple of men too. You should join us." It wasn't until the words were out of her mouth that she realized the invitation might not have been appropriate. It wasn't like they were exactly friends. However, they were no longer enemies. She wasn't exactly sure where it left them.

"I don't know. It sounds like a big commitment."

"It isn't. All you have to do is read one book a month. And our meetings are only once a month, not every week." And there she went again, trying to draw him into her world. She couldn't seem to help herself.

"I'll keep it in mind, but honestly I don't know how much longer I'm going to be on the island."

He was leaving? The thought filled her with sadness. Before she could figure out why she was having any feelings about whether he stayed or left Bluestar, a noise caught her attention.

She stopped walking. "Wait."

He turned to her with a worried look. "What's wrong?"

"Shh..." She held a finger to her lips to keep him from talking.

She didn't hear anything now, but she was certain she'd heard something. It was a whining sound of some sort, but it'd been too brief for her to be able to distinguish the sound.

After a moment, Kent went to speak again, but there was the sound again. He wordlessly closed his mouth as his gaze moved to the beach grass. It was so dark that it was impossible to distinguish anything in the shadows.

"What is that?" he asked.

"I don't know for sure, but it sounds like a kitten."

"What would a kitten be doing all the way out here?"

"I don't know, but we need to find it."

They both turned on the light app on their cell phones. She wasn't leaving there until she knew the kitten was safe. Where was he?

When Sara was young, she would bring home every stray or lost animal that crossed her path. One time she'd even convinced her parents to let her keep a dog.

"What has you so quiet?" he asked.

"You mean other than searching for the kitten that might have run away by now?"

"Yes, other than that."

"If you must know, I was thinking about a stray dog that I found when I was a kid."

"Did you keep him?"

"Of course." She smiled at the memory of him.

"What was his name?"

"Spot."

"That's not very imaginative."

"Hey, I was only seven at the time. I went for the obvious name." She didn't want to delve too far into the past right now. "Now shush. We have to find the kitten."

"I think it's gone now."

She wasn't convinced. There was a lot of thick beach grass. It could just be hunkered down and hiding, but how were they going to find it?

She had an idea. She whispered, "Turn off your light."

"Why?"

"Shush," she whispered. "Just do it."

At the same time, they both turned off their lights. And then they stood there quietly in the dark. In a few moments, there was a high-pitched cry. If she guessed correctly she'd say the little fellow or little girl was hungry and missing their mama.

This time she didn't turn on her light app. Instead, she let her eyes adjust to the darkness and let the moonlight be her guide. She relied heavily on her sense of hearing to guide her. As the kitten cried out again, she zeroed in on its position in the grass. When she finally spotted a ball of black and white fur, she silently signaled to Kent. She didn't want the kitten to get away. It needed help.

Without a plan for what happened next, she lunged for the kitten. When her fingers touched the downy soft fur, she slipped her fingers under its belly and lifted it. The kitten let out fearful cries.

"The poor little guy." She held him to her chest, hoping to comfort him.

The kitten continued to cry and wiggle his legs. His teeny tiny nails got caught in her shirt.

Kent's brows knit together. "What are you going to do with it?"

"I don't know, but I can't leave it out here." The kitten's front claws dug into her hand. It was amazing how sharp they were. They were like little pins.

"Then let's go to your place, and we can figure something out."

He didn't have to tell her twice. She moved past him and headed for her apartment. Luckily, she didn't live far from there. All the while the kitten cried. As it wiggled, she struggled to hold onto it without holding it too tightly. She didn't want to hurt the little fella.

She rushed up the steps to her second-floor apartment. She turned to Kent. "Can you hold him while I unlock the door?" She didn't wait for him to answer. She gently pushed the kitten to his chest. "Be careful not to hold him too tightly." The kitten quieted in Kent's embrace. She was impressed. "He likes you."

"Nah. I just think he's tired of crying."

She unlocked the door. Once inside, she turned on the lights. When she turned around, she almost bumped into Kent. Her mouth grew dry as she stepped back. "Uh...sorry."

"What do you want me to do with him?" He held up the kitten.

"You can put him down on the tile floor in the kitchen." She pointed him in the right direction.

The truth of the matter was that she wasn't prepared to take care of a kitten. She hadn't had a cat since she was little.

When Kent set the kitten on the floor, it began to cry again. He turned to Sara. "What should we do?"

"It needs water, food, and a litter box."

"Do you have all of that?"

"Nope. I don't have a cat." She looked at the kitten as it meandered through her galley kitchen. "I need to run to the store."

She checked the time. There was only one store on the island that stayed open this late. Hopefully, they'd have what she needed. When the kitten attempted to escape the kitchen, she knelt down and picked it up. She turned it around, trying to keep it on the tile floor in case it had an accident.

"Maybe I should go to the store, and you can stay here and keep an eye on it." His gaze searched hers.

"I don't know." She glanced down at the kitten, who looked like it needed a good meal and a bath.

She didn't want to ask him for anything. It totally went against everything in her. This would move them beyond just co-workers. It could possibly put them in the friends category.

The kitten toddled over to her. It stood up on her leg. Its fine needle-like nails pricked her skin. She really needed to take care of the little guy.

She turned to Kent. "Are you sure you don't mind?"

"I didn't have anything else planned for the evening. Just tell me what you need, and I'll get it."

She rattled off a list from kitten food to litter with a number of items in between. And then she gave him some cash. He resisted taking her money, but she insisted.

While he was gone, she got the kitten some water. At first the kitten didn't know what to make of the bowl of water. Sara repeatedly stuck her finger in the water and then dabbed the kitten's nose. The kitten would lick its nose. And then they'd do it again. Eventually, the kitten moved closer to the bowl to check it out.

When the kitten took its first drink, it went at the water too quickly, and its nose went under the water. It jumped back and shook his head, sending water drops flying. It sneezed a couple of times.

But being a very determined kitten, it went back for another drink. It licked at the water. Once again, it got water in its nose. A few sneezes later, and he was back drinking more water.

She sat down on the floor next to the kitten. While she watched it figure out how to drink from a bowl, she reached for her phone. She recalled what Kent had said about her sister keeping a secret. With him at the store, it was time to find out what her sister was keeping from her.

Sara checked the time. It was after nine o'clock. Where her sister was in Malaysia, there was a twelve-hour time difference. She dialed her sister's number. The phone rang and rang. Then it switched to voicemail.

"Hi. This is Cari. I can't talk right now, but if you leave me a message, I'll call you back." Her sister's voice sounded upbeat and cheery.

Sara thought about hanging up, but this was too important. "Hey, it's me. I need to talk to you. Can you give me a call back?"

She disconnected the call. This wasn't the first time they'd missed each other. In fact, it happened frequently. When one of them was up and starting their day, the other was calling it a night.

She glanced down to find the kitten had climbed up onto her lap and made itself comfortable. As Sara ran a finger down over the kitten's back, it let out a loud purr that vibrated its entire body.

"You poor baby. How in the world did you get out there on the beach all by yourself?"

As she watched the kitten, it started to drift off to sleep. Then it would start to fall over. This would startle the kitten and it would wake up.

"It's okay, little guy. You're safe now. I know you're hungry. We'll get you fed and then cleaned up. Just a little longer."

She wasn't sure how much time had passed when Kent returned with all of the supplies Sara had requested. She thanked him and then washed up the kitten's bowl before putting some food in it for the kitten. This time the kitten didn't need any help trying to figure out how to eat. It moved to the bowl and started licking the wet food. It took him no time to eat it all. The kitten's belly was slightly rounded when he finished.

Kent stayed and assisted her as she used some baby shampoo to bathe the kitten. She used a damp paper towel to clean a little goop from its eyes. When the kitten looked at her, she found his eyes were blue. A beautiful blue like the ocean. She wondered if they'd stay that color or change as the kitten grew older.

With the kitten all spiffed up, she cuddled the fluff ball in a towel and held it to her chest. The kitten was either too tired to fight or it felt safe with her because it just settled against her.

"She likes you," Kent said.

"It's not a she."

"What? Are you sure?"

She nodded. "I'm positive."

Kent smiled. "So it's a little boy." He peered closer at the kitten. "A handsome little boy."

"You seem to like him a lot. Would you like to take him home with you?"

Kent immediately shook his head. "I can't have pets at my place."

"Oh."

"What about you? Are you allowed pets here?"

"Yes, but it has to be a cat or a small dog."

"Then it looks like you're all set. I set up the litter box in the bathroom like you wanted."

"Thank you for everything. I don't know what I would have done if you hadn't been here to help me."

"I'm sure you would have figured something out. Looks like he fell asleep."

Sara glanced down at the kitten in the fluffy peach-colored towel. Its eyes were closed and with each deep breath, his sides expanded. He looked so adorable. But it wasn't staying—at least not for long. She'd deal with getting it home in the morning.

Kent moved toward the door. "Do you need anything else before I go?"

She shook her head. "I've got it from here."

Kent's gaze lowered to the kitten again. "He certainly looks content. What are you going to call him? You can't keep calling him kitten."

She shook her head. "I'm not naming him."

"Why not?"

"Because a name denotes an attachment. And I'm not going to get attached to this kitten, because soon he'll be going home."

Kent arched a brow. "You sound so certain."

"I am. He must have gotten lost is all."

Kent didn't look so certain. "He was awfully dirty and hungry for just being lost."

He had a point, but she wasn't willing to admit it to herself or him. "I'll deal with it all in the morning."

"Okay. If you need anything just call me."

That was sweet of him. "Thanks. But I don't have your number."

His gaze moved to the kitchen counter. "Do you mind if I put it in your phone?"

"Not at all." The words were out of her mouth before she realized he was once again breaching the wall that she had up between them. It was her tiredness. She just needed some sleep, and then everything would go back to normal.

Once Kent input his number in her phone, he told her goodnight and then paused to pet the kitten before he walked out the door.

She stood there for a moment at the top of the steps, watching him walk away. She'd seen a totally different side of Kent that evening. After seeing this friendly, caring side of him, it was so hard to envision him as the jerk who'd hurt her sister. In fact, it was easy to envision them becoming friends.

She inwardly groaned. She really wished her sister would call her back so she would have some answers. When she went back inside the apartment, she checked her phone. There was no message from Cari. With a groan, Sara put the phone back on the counter. What was this secret that Kent said wasn't his to share?

CHAPTER NINE

S HE WAS LATE FOR work.

Sara was never late for work—not until now. Her tardiness was due to the kitten. It kept crying off and on during the night. She kept doing everything she could think of to comfort it. The only time it was quiet was when she held it, but she couldn't do that all day. She had to go to work.

And of course, when she checked her phone that morning, she'd found her sister had called her back. But with the kitten to deal with, she'd left her phone on the kitchen counter during the night, and she hadn't heard it from her bedroom. It appeared they were once again going to play a game of phone tag.

When she'd called on her way to work, she'd gotten her sister's voicemail once again. This time she didn't leave a message. There was no point. One of these times, they'd connect.

She'd worried about leaving the kitten home alone, so she'd asked her next-door neighbor Birdie if she could keep an eye on it. And that had taken more time because she couldn't have Birdie climbing the steps to her second-floor apartment. So she'd had to carry all of the kitten supplies over to Birdie's place, but she felt so much better knowing someone was keeping an eye on the kitten while it was still figuring things out.

The morning was crazy busy with guests checking out and other guests checking in. And housekeeping was short-staffed so that meant calling in a couple of people on their day off. Plus, the laundry they outsourced was delivered, but they weren't the inn's linens. If that wasn't enough, the internet went down. She made a call to the island's provider only to find out there wasn't a problem on their end, so they'd send someone over to scout the problem.

By lunchtime, she was exhausted. But she didn't have time to rest because she had to find the kitten's home. She had taken a bunch of photos of the furbaby that morning. Now she just had to pick the best one.

"Looks like you're busy today." Kent's voice startled her.

She spun around to find him leaning against the counter in the temporary lobby. "Sorry. I didn't hear you approach."

"What has you so preoccupied?"

She held out her phone with a picture of the kitten. "I took more than a dozen photos and I'm trying to pick out the best one."

A smile pulled at her lips as she flipped through the photos. The kitten had been curious about her camera, and so there was a closeup photo of the kitten nosing her phone.

Kent peered over her shoulder, looking at the kitten pictures. "How's your search for the owner coming?"

"I was just working on it." She swiped right on her phone and held up another photo of the kitten. "Do you think that will work for a lost kitten post on social media?"

He nodded. "Looks good to me."

"Great." Her fingers moved over the phone's screen as she uploaded the post to the island's message board. "Done."

"You might want to print up some flyers."

"Do you really think it's necessary?"

"A number of the older folks on the island aren't much into the internet. Trust me, I know because of the advertising I do for the furniture store."

"Okay. I can do that." She logged into the computer at the reception desk and set to work. Five minutes later, she had some flyers printed up. A frown pulled at her face.

"What's wrong?"

She lowered her voice. "You aren't going to tell anyone that I used the work computer to do my personal stuff, are you?"

His brows lifted. "You would get in trouble for that?"

She shrugged. "Josie is pretty easygoing, but there is a rule about not doing personal stuff on the computers."

"So you're a rule breaker. Who'd have thought it?" He smiled and shook his head.

A frown pulled at the corner of her lips. "This isn't funny. I'm serious. I can't afford to get in trouble."

The smile disappeared from his face. "Okay. I promise I won't say anything, but I really don't think it's that big of a deal."

"Thank you." She grabbed the printouts from the color printer.

"Well, can you afford a lunch break?"

She checked her fitness watch. "I don't have long."

"I'll tell you what, we'll make this a working lunch."

"How's that?"

"We'll put up the flyers on our way to lunch."

She shrugged. "Okay."

And so they set off. Since she walked to work, they took Kent's cart to save time. When they got into town, they would stop periodically and use a staple gun Kent had grabbed from his toolbox to put a flyer on a utility pole.

While he did that, she stepped into the dress shop and asked if they'd keep the flyer by the register. They happily agreed. She loved how helpful the residents of Bluestar could be. She was lucky to call this place home.

When she exited the shop, she almost ran into someone. She stopped short and glanced up. "Oh. Hello."

Mayor Tony Banks frowned. He wasn't much older than her, but his persona was one of a much older, proper gentleman, especially with his bowties. Where in the world did he get the idea to wear a bowtie every day?

He was definitely one of the more unique people on the island. He was still a bachelor, and Sara could see why. It would take someone strong enough to loosen him up before he'd be ready to settle down.

Mayor Banks's gaze lowered to the flyers in her hand. "So, it's you that's putting those up all around town."

"Yes, sir." *Ugh.* Had she really just called him sir? She swallowed hard. "I just want to get the kitten home where he belongs. I hope the flyers aren't a problem."

The mayor hesitated, making her wonder if he was going to make her take them all down. "Just don't forget to take them down when the owner is located."

"I won't. I promise." The man made her so nervous.

Kent joined them. "Is there a problem?"

"No," Sara said quickly. "The mayor was just making sure we remember to take the flyers down once the kitten's owners are located."

Kent's gaze moved to Mayor Banks. "Hey, Tony, how's it going?"

"Just trying to stay on top of things. With the Concert on the Beach coming up, there are a lot of preparations to see to." The mayor's gaze moved between the two of them. "Are you two going to the concert?"

"Uh…I don't know." Sara's gaze moved to Kent's.

He shrugged. "I hadn't thought about it."

The mayor frowned at their lack of enthusiasm for the event. "You both should go. It's going to be spectacular. You should check out the lineup. It's even more impressive than last year." And then he continued on down the sidewalk.

Kent leaned over and whispered, "Between you and me, I didn't go last year."

"You didn't? I thought everyone was there. It felt like it with the massive crowd. You should check it out this year." Her gaze moved to him. "So, what do you say?"

"About what?"

"Going to the concert together?"

His brows rose. "Are you asking me on a date?"

"What?" Her voice rose a couple of octaves as the heat rushed to her cheeks. "No. Of course not. I just thought we could go as you know, friends...and, uh, celebrate finishing the lobby." As he continued to stare at her, she became even more flustered. "You know what, never mind. It was a bad idea."

He let out a laugh. "We'll see how it goes. If we get our work done on time, perhaps I could meet you at say seven on that Saturday night."

"Sounds good. Where do you want to meet?"

"I don't know."

She gave it a little thought. "How about at the sandcastle sculpture in the park?"

He nodded. "I'll see you there."

They continued distributing the flyers around town. Lots of people inquired about the kitten, but none of them knew where he belonged, and they'd promised to let her know if they learned anything.

"I know," Sara said. "We should put a flyer up on the bulletin board at the Lighthouse Café."

"And instead of going to Hamming It Up for sandwiches, we can just grab some lunch at the Lighthouse."

"Sounds good to me."

A few minutes later, they were seated in a booth at the café. They were lucky to get the only available table. The place was hopping. And if a couple hadn't just vacated the spot, they'd still be waiting by the door. In fact, they had snagged the spot before the staff even had a chance to clear the table and reset it. But she didn't have time to waste, and Kent hadn't seemed to mind.

Once the table was reset and they'd had a chance to look at the menu, she ordered a chicken salad with fries, and he ordered a cheeseburger with a side fries. She pulled her phone from her purse and placed it on the table. There were no messages or missed calls. She sighed. She wasn't good at waiting on things.

Kent leaned back on the bench. "Did you really think someone would have seen your flyer already?"

"You can't blame me for hoping. And I've been playing phone tag with my sister. It's her turn to call. I hate how hard it is to stay in contact."

He arched a brow. "Are you worried about her?"

Sara was quiet for a moment as she carefully considered her answer. She didn't want to repeat their earlier conversation. She knew that it would lead nowhere. And even if he did break down and tell her what had happened with him and Cari, would she believe him?

Sara studied him for a moment. The answer startled her. She would believe him. But she knew as sure as the sun would come up tomorrow that he would keep his word to her sister and whatever had happened would remain a secret.

It was best she stuck to subjects that were less likely to strike up a conflict between them since they had to work together if they wanted to complete the lobby in time for the wedding.

She arranged the flatware on the paper placemat. "I guess I'm just curious about why she's suddenly moving home."

"So you think something is wrong?"

Sara shook her head. "No. She's been so busy lately that this phone tag thing we're doing has become a normal part of our routine. I know she teaches, but that can't possibly take up all of her time. So, I just wonder what else she's been doing?"

"Did you ever think she might have met someone?"

Sara opened her mouth, but then she wordlessly closed it again. Why hadn't she thought of that? Probably because Cari never mentioned meeting anyone. If this were true, it was yet another example of them not telling each other everything.

She was starting to wonder if they were as close as she'd always thought them to be. Or was it just something she made up in her mind after their mother died? Did she try to make up for such a great loss by creating this amazing bond with her sister that didn't really exist except in her own mind?

"Hey." Kent's voice drew her from her thoughts. "Would it really be so bad if she found someone?"

Sara shook her head instead of speaking. She wasn't sure if in that moment she trusted her voice. The thought of her sister shutting her out of her life drove a painful wedge into her heart.

Thankfully, they were distracted with the delivery of their food. Whereas she was starving when they'd walked in the door, now her appetite was waning.

When Kent noticed she wasn't eating, he asked, "Is there something wrong with your food?"

She shook her head and stabbed a lettuce leaf with her fork. After she ate it, she decided to change the subject to the lobby project and what they needed to accomplish that day.

—*ell*—

It had been a long day.

And yet Sara's company had definitely been the highlight.

Kent was impressed with the work they'd gotten done so far. The walls were painted and that left the trim work that needed to be done. The progress was slower than he'd been hoping, but so far they were on track to have it completed in time for the wedding.

Ding.

He pulled his phone out of his back pocket. It was a message from his sister.

Josie: How's it going?
Kent: Good. I think you'll really like the new look.
Josie: I better. Or else you're in trouble.

He smiled and shook his head. Leave it to his sister to complain about free labor. But he knew she was just giving him grief like a little sister is prone to do.

Kent: How's the trip?

Josie: Great. Lane has been showing me around.
Kent: Have fun.
Josie: I am. Send me pictures of the lobby.
Kent: No. It's going to be a surprise.
Josie: Pretty please.
Kent: Nope. Don't worry. It'll look fantastic.
Josie: *frowning emoji* I'm counting on it.

He just hoped it *would* look fantastic. Without the floor in and the trim work not done, it was so hard to tell if this was going to turn out the way he'd envisioned. Even if it didn't, he'd do whatever it took to make it look good.

Sara had been worried about the kitten being with Birdie for too long, so he sent her home an hour ago. There was just some trim work that he wanted to finish up. Even though there wasn't nearly as much trim to paint versus the walls, it was taking him two or three times as long to paint it because of the grooves and trying not to get the bright white paint on the walls. Perhaps he should have done the trim before he painted the walls. He'd keep that in mind for the next time—if there was a next time.

He was quickly realizing that this refresh project was a lot more involved than he'd originally imagined. There was no way he could keep his office job at the store and do the refresh work. He would have to make a choice.

To complicate matters, he was already exploring job opportunities on the mainland. After all, his older brother, Grant, lived in Boston. It wasn't like he wouldn't have any family around. And Kent had just received a call from a potential employer.

It was a lot to think about. And he had only twelve days to make up his mind. He was determined to have a decision by the end of his vacation. He just didn't know what that decision would be—at least not yet.

With all of the supplies taken care of, he was ready to call it a night. He was just about to turn off the lights when he noticed Sara had forgotten her phone. He knew she must be going crazy trying to find it.

He picked it up. He'd drop it off at her place on his way home. It was nice to have an excuse to stop by her place. He assured himself it was just the kitten he was looking forward to seeing—not the beautiful woman who was caring for the kitten.

In his cart, it didn't take him long to get to Sara's place. The sun was already sinking low in the horizon. As he made his way up her steps, he was amazed at the fantastic view she had. If it wouldn't have seemed strange, he would have stood on her porch and stared out at the colorful sunset that was sending color cascading over the water.

With the greatest of regret, he turned to her door and knocked. He heard something crash inside, followed by an *oof!* What in the world?

"I'll be right there," Sara called out.

He couldn't help but wonder what was going on inside. A minute or so later, the door opened. Sara looked tired. And her usually perfectly styled hair was a bit mussed up.

"Oh. Hi." She sent him a smile, but it didn't go all the way to her eyes. She tucked a few of the dark strands of hair behind her ear. "You didn't happen to see my phone at the inn, did you?"

He pulled it from his pocket. "Do you mean this phone?"

Her whole face lit up, and her eyes twinkled with happiness. "Thank goodness. I've been ripping this place apart, searching for it. I thought I'd dropped it when I was hauling the kitten's things back from Birdie's." And then as though she realized her manners, she backed up and opened the door wide. "Come on in before the kitten gets out."

He stepped inside and closed the door behind him. He glanced around and spotted the kitten all curled up on a blanket on the couch, sound asleep. Apparently Sara wasn't the only one who was tired.

"Thank you so much for dropping off my phone. I feel so guilty that you had to come over here to give it to me."

"Because it was all of what, a three-minute drive from the inn? Don't worry about it. I know how much you're anticipating a call from the kitten's owner." As he noticed her checking her calls, he asked, "Did you hear anything?"

She shook her head. "My usually busy phone didn't have one phone call this evening." She sighed. "Is it possible the kitten doesn't have a home?"

His gaze moved from Sara to the couch, where the kitten looked quite content. "I don't know if I would say that."

Her gaze followed his. "Oh no. I'm not keeping him."

"Why not?"

Her mouth opened and then closed wordlessly as though she were struggling to find a legitimate reason not to keep the kitten. Then she said, "I'm not home much."

"Not that I know much about cats, but I think they're pretty self-sufficient. And you said your landlord allows cats. Sounds like you're all set."

She frowned at him. "You know you could take him."

Kent shook his head. "I can't have pets at my place, remember?"

Her frown deepened. "You could move."

He let out a laugh. "You want me to find a new place to live on an island with limited housing just so I can take a cat that looks immensely happy with you. I don't think so. When I move, it's going to be to the mainland."

Her fine eyebrows rose. "You're moving?"

He hadn't meant to say anything. "It's a possibility."

"How much of a possibility?"

"As of this afternoon, I got a phone interview."

Her brown eyes lit up with interest. "What does that mean?"

"It means they're supposed to call me back in the next day or two and let me know if I move onto the next round."

"What's the next round?"

"An in-person interview."

"I'm sure you'll make it to the next round. What's the position?"

"It's in public accounting. It's some auditing work like I did fresh out of college before I returned to the island to work in the family business, but there's a lot of room for me to move up. It could provide me with the opportunity to live abroad."

Knock-knock.

He couldn't help but wonder who it would be at this hour. Was it possible Sara had a boyfriend? Then he recalled her telling him that she wasn't in a relationship. Maybe it was a brand-new relationship.

The thought caused a slow burn in his gut. It was an unfamiliar feeling and one he wasn't inclined to examine too closely. What Sara did was her own business. It was absolutely none of his. And yet he didn't make any motion to leave.

Sara stepped around him in order to answer the door. While she did that, he made his way over to the couch. He knelt down in order to pet the kitten.

His fingertips touched the downy soft fur as he stroked the kitten's back. The little one lifted his head, blinked his eyes at him, and then yawned. It appeared the kitten had gotten over its fear of humans. That was good.

Kent lifted his head to see a man on the other side of the door. He looked familiar, but he couldn't readily put a name to the face. The man was holding a pizza box. Sara took it from him and placed it on the kitchen counter.

She grabbed some money and returned to the door. The delivery guy didn't seem in any hurry to leave. He just kept standing there, even after Sara handed him the money. The man was smiling at Sara. And then there was something said that Kent couldn't hear, and the man broke out into a bit of laughter. Was he flirting with her? Kent straightened and made his way to the door. When the guy saw Kent, his eyes momentarily widened as though he were surprised to find Sara with a man. The man excused himself and then hustled down the steps.

She closed the door and turned to Kent. "I didn't know you were coming or I would have ordered more pizza, but I think there's still enough for us to share."

"Thanks. But I need to be going." Deep inside there was a part of him that wanted to stay and hang out, but he knew nothing good would have come from it because she still didn't trust him.

She walked him to the door, and they said a quick goodbye. As he made his way down the steps, he started to regret his decision. Would it have hurt to stay and share some pizza? Probably not.

Every now and then he would catch her looking at him and not in a good way. The look on her face would be one of skepticism or frustration. He knew she was still hung up on what had gone down between him and her sister.

He wanted to tell her it wasn't what she thought—that they hadn't had a summertime love affair—far from it. He wanted to tell her that in his misguided way, he had been trying to help out a friend. But would Sara believe him?

It didn't matter because he'd made a promise to Cari, and he intended to keep it. Even if it meant that Sara kept giving him strange looks and never trusted him. He'd learned a long time ago that if you didn't stand by your word, then you aren't much of a man.

CHAPTER TEN

O NE DAY TURNED INTO two.

And two days turned into three.

Sara stood in the middle of the lobby and looked around at all of their hard work. Well, most of it was Kent's handiwork, but she'd helped out here and there.

As she took it all in, even without the furniture, the refresh was exactly what this place needed. It was a lot lighter and brighter with the new paint and the lighter-colored flooring. She hoped Josie would be as pleased with the transformation as she was.

She also realized her time working with Kent was quickly coming to an end. The furniture was to be delivered the next day. And in a week, they'd be in the midst of final preparations for the Carrington wedding.

The feeling of disappointment over the refresh coming to an end surprised her. During their time together, she'd found that her initial instincts about Kent were correct. He was a really nice guy. So how had things gone so terribly wrong between him and her sister?

She was still playing phone tag with her sister. Cari had left her a message that said she was off exploring, whatever that meant, and that where she was going the cell phone service was spotty at best. She said she would call her as soon as she got back to the city. The only problem was that Cari didn't say when she was getting back to the city.

While Kent was in town picking up a couple additional boxes of flooring, she was supposed to be sketching out a new layout for the display cases as well as the new furniture that was to be delivered in the morning.

She grabbed a tablet and pencil from one of the offices and started to draw. Instead of having all of Bluestar's memorabilia on one side of the lobby, she set about spreading out the photos and displays. It would allow for more people to have access to the displays.

As the pencil moved over the pad, she frowned. She just didn't like the way the furniture was positioned. And so she flipped to a fresh page and started again. This time she didn't put in all of the display cases and furniture. Instead, she put in a couple of displays and then a couple pieces of furniture. It was a bit of a game of Tetris to get all of the pieces to fit together in a cohesive fashion.

She found herself enjoying this sort of work. In fact, the more she worked on the final vision for the room, the more ideas she got. She turned to the windows. They were large and let in a lot of light, but some sheers would soften them without blocking the light. She made a note of her idea. She also jotted down other things to discuss with Kent: a throw rug, runner, potted plants, an artificial tree or two, twinkle lights, and some large coffee table books.

Buzz-buzz.

She wondered if it was Kent. Perhaps he'd run into a problem getting the flooring. When she retrieved the phone from her pocket, she was surprised and delighted to find the call was from her sister. At last, they'd connected.

She pressed the phone to her ear. "Hey, I was beginning to think we'd never get to talk to each other again."

"Sorry about that. The phone service was terrible, but the trip was amazing."

"Sounds like you had a good time."

"I did." Cari told her a little about her trip into the countryside and the amazing things she'd seen and experienced.

There was a part of Sara that was happy for her sister and another part that was a little bit jealous that her sister was out there experiencing all of these new adventures. Sometimes she wondered why she remained on the island. Everyone else that she loved had left her. Her parents had passed on much too soon. Her best friend in school had moved to Oregon. She rarely heard from her. And her sister had up and left to follow her dreams halfway around the world. Sara didn't know why the people she loved the most always left her.

But there was something grounding about Bluestar Island. It gave her a sense of belonging—of the locals being part of her extended family. And maybe that had to be enough for her because even though she casually dated, she never let things get serious, because she knew the relationship would never last—nothing in her life ever did. That was why she was so desperate to impress Josie. She wanted her job at the inn to be the one thing in her life that lasted—she wanted it to be something she could count on.

"So what did you want to talk about?" Her sister's voice drew Sara from her thoughts.

Sara wasn't sure where to start. She definitely didn't want to dive right into the part about her working with Kent. Or the part where they'd shared a meal, and he'd helped her with the kitten. As she thought of it all, she realized that this past week they'd spent most of their time together.

Sara swallowed hard and started with the part about Josie going out of town and how she was an acting manager while she was away.

"And that's what was so urgent that you kept calling me?" There was skepticism in her sister's voice.

"No. Not exactly."

"Is this about the apartment?" A hopeful tone replaced the skepticism.

"Actually, it kind of is."

"I'm confused. Does this mean you secured an apartment for me?"

"Not exactly." Sara inwardly groaned. Now that she was talking to her sister, all of her well-rehearsed words fled her. And she wasn't sure how to phrase this without upsetting her sister. "The thing is that in order to get the apartment for you, I had to make a deal."

"What sort of deal?"

This was the sticky part. She had absolutely no idea how her sister would react to her working so closely with her ex. The very last thing Sara wanted was for her sister to be mad at her. "It doesn't matter."

"Sara, what have you done?" Her sister used the same tone of voice that she had when they were kids and Sara had done something wrong.

"Nothing except get you a place to live." Sara was growing frustrated with her sister. Instead of her being grateful that she'd done everything she could to make it possible for Cari to move home, she was acting like Sara had done something wrong. "Why don't you tell me what happened to break up you and Kent?"

"That was a long time ago." An awkward silence ensued. "I...I can't remember. Besides, it's not important."

She couldn't remember? Seriously? Did Cari really think she was going to believe that story? After all, it wasn't that long ago. She was certain her sister knew exactly what had happened.

"I think it is important." Sara's words were direct because she just couldn't keep up the struggle of keeping Kent at arm's length if she didn't know exactly why she was doing it. "What went down between you and him? Why did he dump you?"

Her sister grew quiet. So quiet that for a moment she thought the phone went dead. Then Cari said, "Is this really that important to you?"

"It is. Very much so."

Cari sighed. "A group of friends went to the mainland. We were planning to have a good time. Have some dinner, go to a concert, and then head back to the island. Kent was one of the people in our group."

"Was he your date?"

"No. Just a friend. We were all just friends." She drew in an uneven breath. Her words came a bit slower, and there was some distance as though her sister's thoughts were drawn back to that time. "Dinner was fine. In fact, we were having a really good time. And then we went to the concert."

Sara had no idea where her sister was going with this story, and so she quietly waited. She hoped Kent hadn't done anything wrong. She really hoped that. The degree with which she longed for Kent to be a good guy in this story shocked her. Since when had she grown from being upset with him for hurting her sister to caring about him?

"I had to use the ladies' room. When I was coming out, I forgot my way back to our seats. After I ran into an attendant and got pointed in the right direction, I started back along the outer corridor. Someone grabbed me and pulled me into the shadows." There was a distinct pause as though she had gotten lost in her thoughts.

The breath caught in Sara's throat. She couldn't believe what she was hearing. Her sister had been attacked?

"The guy... He, uh, hit me a few times and ripped my clothes." The pain in her voice was evident.

She should say something, but her throat muscles refused to work. This was so much worse than she'd imagined. How had this happened and she didn't know about it? Why hadn't her sister leaned on her?

"Kent had been on his way to the men's room when he heard me scream. He stopped the guy from...from attacking me."

Thank goodness. "I'm so sorry that happened to you. I had no idea."

"I didn't want you to know."

Her admission arrowed into Sara's heart. She had absolutely no idea her sister had been assaulted.

"Why didn't you tell me? We're sisters. I thought we shared everything."

"After losing Mom, I...I didn't feel like we could share everything. You had your own stuff you were going through. And I didn't want you to think you couldn't come to me with your problems."

As much as she wanted to be angry with her sister, she also knew that Cari had stepped into the parent role in her life after their mother died. With no mother and a father who barely functioned in his unending grief, Cari was all she'd had to make sure she had food to eat, clean clothes to wear, and to make sure she didn't go off and do something stupid.

A new sense of gratitude and a deepening love for her sister swept over Sara. "I wish I could have been there for you. You were always there for me."

"It's okay. When they didn't catch the guy, I freaked out. The only people who knew were Kent and the police. And that's the way I wanted it. But then I got afraid to go out and do things."

Sara searched her memory. It took some thinking, but then she recalled a period Cari wouldn't go out of the house. She'd made up excuse after excuse. Sara had thought it was strange at the time, but she'd been home from college on summer break and working part-time at the inn.

She felt sick in the stomach upon realizing what her sister had been going through. "I'm so sorry."

"You have nothing to be sorry for."

"But I am." She loved her sister and would do anything for her. "I was so caught up in my own life that I didn't even realize what was going on with you."

"You were young. That's the way it was supposed to be. And I was all right."

"Really?" She didn't believe her. "I wouldn't have been. That must have been so horrendous."

There was a pause. "It was. But I got through it."

She hated that her sister was half a globe away, and she couldn't put her arms around her. This moment required something more than words because her words felt so inadequate. Sara sucked down her rising emotions. Her sister didn't need to deal with that right now.

She swallowed hard. "And that's how you started dating Kent?"

"You see, about that, um... We never really dated."

Sara's mouth opened, but no words came out. She had too many thoughts rising in her mind and crashing into each other. It was hard to capture just one concrete thought. "I don't understand."

"Kent was worried about me. And looking back on it now, he had every reason to worry. I think in the beginning I was in shock."

Sara's heart ached for her sister. And she hated that Cari thought she had to go through all of this by herself. Sara leaned against the wall before sinking down to the floor. "But I don't understand. It seemed like you and Kent were together most of that summer."

Cari sighed. "At first, he'd stop by to check on me. He wanted me to tell people, but I refused. So, he finally talked me into going to see a counselor. It was the best thing for me."

Wow. So Kent was actually a hero. The news was such a welcome relief, but then she thought back to how she'd treated him after he'd supposedly dumped her sister. It wasn't right of her. She owed him a really big apology.

"And then when he noticed I was spending all of my time in the house because I wasn't comfortable going out in public alone, even on the island, he escorted me. He was super great to me. I don't think I'll ever be able to repay him. If it wasn't for him, I never would have been able to travel to Malaysia and work here."

Her sister's explanation answered so many questions in Sara's mind. "But what about your big breakup? If you weren't dating, how could you break up? I'm confused."

"I knew Kent liked someone, but he wouldn't ask them out because he was spending all of his time with me. I finally felt confident enough to go it alone. When I told him that, he asked what we were going to tell people. And since the rumor mill in Bluestar had already jumped to the conclusion that we were dating, we decided to let them jump to the conclusion that we'd broken up."

"You never liked him that way?" The breath caught in Sara's lungs as she awaited her sister's answer.

"No. Not at all. He was a great friend when I needed one." There was a pause while Sara absorbed this information, and then Cari said, "You like him, don't you?"

"No." The answer came out too fast and too emphatically. She inwardly groaned. It didn't even sound truthful to her own ears.

"Uh-huh."

She could envision her sister wearing a sure-you-don't smile. "Stop."

"What? I'm not doing anything."

"You're grinning. I know it."

Her sister let out a laugh. It was so good to hear that after the emotional conversation. Her sister had gone through something horrible, but thanks to Kent being her friend and helping her, Cari was doing all right.

"You know it's all right if you want to date Kent," Cari said with all sincerity.

Just then she heard a noise behind her. She turned around and found Kent returning with the supplies he'd gone to get in town. He went to say something but must have seen the phone in her hand because he wordlessly closed his mouth and went about putting the new supplies with the others.

"Thanks." Sara got to her feet. "I've got to run. I love you."

"Love you too."

She slipped the phone into her pocket. Thank goodness he hadn't returned any sooner and overheard any of the conversation. She didn't want him to know they'd been talking about him or that the subject of her dating him had come up.

She owed him a big apology for being such a jerk to him in the past. She thought of just going up to him and uttering "I'm sorry," but she didn't think that was sufficient. She'd give it some more thought.

CHAPTER ELEVEN

S OMETHING WAS DIFFERENT.

Kent couldn't put his finger on what had changed with Sara, but something definitely had. He paused from where he was putting in the last bit of flooring. He heard something. For a moment, he couldn't make it out, but then he realized it was Sara, and she was humming. He didn't think he'd ever heard her hum before.

He didn't know what had put her in such a good mood, but he hoped it continued. He glanced over at her just as she looked in his direction. Their gazes connected and held longer than they should have.

His heart thumped. He was drawn to her in a way that he'd never been drawn to another person. It went beyond her silky black hair, which he longed to comb his fingers through, or her honey-brown eyes, which he could get lost in. Her beauty started so much deeper with her kind heart and her thoughtfulness, and it radiated outward.

And yet he knew he couldn't let himself get close to her. It was hard enough moving away from the island with most of his family here, but to get involved with her at this point would make leaving nearly impossible. And he wasn't ready to settle with life the way it was with no say at the store and being constantly vetoed by his ever-cautious parents.

He had to break out of this routine he'd let himself get drawn into when his parents told him that he'd be their partner and have a say in the business. He'd since learned that he didn't think his parents ever intended to retire. They loved going to the store each day and talking with the townspeople. It was more of a social circle for them than a business. And they didn't want any of it to change. And that was fine. It was their business. He truly wanted to see them happy. It was just that he also wanted to find his own happiness.

The reminder of his situation had him looking away. No matter how attractive he found Sara or how much he might like to spend more time with her, when this job was over, they would go their separate ways. Not that they could go that far from each other on this small island, but they wouldn't be spending hours together each day.

With that thought in mind, he worked faster. The sooner the job was finished, the sooner the temptation would lessen. The rubber mallet he was using to fit the flooring in snugly missed and hit him instead.

"Is everything okay?" Concern rang out in Sara's voice.

He inwardly groaned. So she'd seen him being an utter klutz. "Um, yes. I'm just trying to get this floor finished."

Sara moved to stand next to him. "This place is starting to look really good."

He glanced up. "You sound surprised."

Color filled her cheeks. "I am. It just seemed like this was all spontaneous, and I wasn't sure how it was going to turn out."

"Well, it would look a lot better if you'd give me a hand with this floor."

She arched a brow. "You think so, huh?"

When she smiled at him, it gave him a funny feeling deep within his chest. It was something he'd never experienced before. And something told him it was best not to examine those feelings too closely.

Sara grabbed a piece of flooring and set to work. He had to admit that working with her was preferable to working alone. In fact, if he wasn't careful, he could get quite used to this arrangement.

What should she do?

It'd been the question Sara had been asking herself ever since she'd finished her conversation with her sister. She wanted so badly to make things up to Kent, but nothing seemed like it would be enough. Maybe she just had to start small and keep showing him that she felt awful for misreading what had gone down between him and her sister.

Even with an apology, she knew it might not change things between them. And that was all on her. Still, she had to do something.

Their refresh project was quickly coming to an end. Although they both lived on this small island, their circle of friends didn't intersect. They would go back to occasionally bumping into each other on the streets of Bluestar. She wanted something more than that, but she didn't know what that might look like.

She realized there was no better time to set her plan into motion than right now—this very moment—before she lost her nerve.

She swallowed hard. "Kent, would you like to grab some dinner?" When he sent her a blank stare, as though unsure of what exactly she meant, she said, "You know...together."

He didn't say a word for a moment, as though her dinner request had caught him off guard. But it wasn't like they hadn't shared a meal before. And then she realized that in those past cases, he'd been the one doing the asking.

"Um...sure." He cleared his throat. "I guess."

His hesitation made her stomach knot up. Still she forced a smile to her lips. "How about I cook us something?"

"Oh, okay. What can I bring?"

"Yourself." Worried that he might back out, she said, "I'll see you at seven."

And then she made her way out the door. She didn't dare glance over her shoulder. She didn't want to give him a chance to say that he'd changed his mind. Not that she could blame him. She hadn't been that nice to him in the past. She'd like to think that while they'd been working together, they had given not only the room a refresh but also their relationship. She truly smiled. *Hey, not only rooms can use a refresh.*

She walked straight home instead of taking the scenic route on the beach. She'd been doing that ever since she found the kitten. Now that the kitten was acclimating to her apartment, she'd been leaving the kitten home alone. So far things appeared to be going well. She still hated leaving the kitten alone all day. Well, not quite all day because she tried to pop in each day at lunchtime to make sure the kitten was all right. And since she was there, she'd feed him some wet food for lunch. A growing kitty needed his nourishment.

Not that she was getting attached. She knew one day soon the kitten would go home. Sara told herself that was fine. She didn't need another responsibility. She had plenty of them already at the inn.

Still, it was so nice to come home to someone again. It felt like forever since her sister had up and moved away. Sara thought she'd adjusted to living alone, but the kitten was proving that wasn't quite the case.

Sara bounded up the steps to her second-floor apartment. As soon as she opened the door and stepped inside, the kitty leapt off the couch, yawned, and stretched. And then he ran toward Sara, but with his short little legs, the running looked more like a bunny hop. He was *sooo* cute. It made Sara's heart swoon every time the kitten greeted her.

Sara scooped up the kitten. His front paws climbed up Sara's shoulder. The kitten rubbed his fuzzy head along Sara's jaw.

Sara ran her hand gently down the kitten's back. The kitty's purr was so loud for a little kitten. It vibrated throughout his tiny body. Sara's smile broadened. Someone would be very lucky to call this kitten their own. Sara kissed the top of the kitten's head before placing him back on the floor. "Sorry. I have to make dinner."

As she tried to make her way to the kitchen, the kitten kept rubbing against her ankles. At one point, Sara tripped because the kitten insisted on walking in circles around Sara's legs. Luckily, Sara was able to reach out for the post at the end of the kitchen's island and regain her balance.

Once she was standing still, the kitten began to climb her jeans. His needle-like nails pierced her pants and dug into her leg. "Ouch!"

Sara bent over and picked up the kitten. It took a moment to release the kitten's nails from the material. Once the kitten was free, Sara lifted her up until they were face to face. "I know you missed me. I missed you too. But we're going to have company for dinner."

"Meow."

"Ah, so you like the thought of company. You'll be even happier to know that it's Kent."

"Meow-meow."

"How about I make you a deal? I'll give you some food, and then you can take a nap on the couch while I make something for Kent to eat."

"Meow."

"Good. I knew you'd see it my way." She hugged the kitten before placing him on the floor.

Sara didn't waste any time getting the kitten some food. She knew if she took her time, she'd end up with the kitten climbing up her leg again. And it hurt, a lot. Once the kitten was fed, Sara realized she had no idea what to make for dinner. It was a good thing she'd stopped and picked up some groceries yesterday. Now to decide what she would make.

It had to be something a little bit impressive. And yet it needed to be something that wasn't too elaborate. He would be there within the hour.

CHAPTER TWELVE

W HAT WAS GOING ON?

Kent couldn't believe Sara had invited him to her place for dinner. It was almost like they were friends. Was that possible? Had she finally gotten over the past?

He wanted to think they were truly friends, but he was hesitant. He knew how she'd falsely believed he'd hurt her sister when in fact it had been quite the opposite. And as much as he'd wanted to explain all of this to her, he just couldn't go back on the promise he'd made to Cari.

Was it possible that by working together, day in and day out, that Sara realized he wasn't the horrible person she'd imagined him to be? He hoped so.

He'd rushed home. His apartment was in the center of Bluestar. As he stepped in the door, he realized it wasn't nearly as nice as Sara's place. Where she had landscape prints on her walls, he hadn't bothered to hang anything on his. He didn't spend much time here. Most of his time was spent at the store and half the time he had dinner with his parents because his mother always cooked more than enough, and he wasn't that anxious to go home and cook for one.

Maybe he'd just let his life get stuck in a rut. The more he thought about it, the more he realized that was exactly what had happened. If he didn't do something about it, nothing was ever going to change. It was in that moment that he promised himself if he got the in-person interview, he'd give it his best try. It would be the first step to changing his life.

He grabbed a quick shower before putting on some fresh clothes. Wanting to build on whatever this dinner represented, he stopped on his way to her place and bought a couple of things to take with him. After all, he wanted to make a good impression.

When he reached the steps leading to Sara's apartment, he paused. He reminded himself this wasn't a date—not even close. This was just Sara being friendly. Nothing more.

And yet there was a part of him that wanted it to be more. So much more. He halted his thoughts. That wasn't going to happen.

He started up the steps. His steps came quickly, and in no time he was rapping his knuckles on the white door.

"Just a minute!"

A minute later, Sara swung the door open. She bestowed on him a brilliant smile. It was so warm it was like standing in front of the afternoon sun. He basked in her friendly gesture.

It took him a moment to remember he'd picked up a bouquet of flowers for her. He held out the arrangement of white roses, pink Gerbera daisies, and green Fuji spider mums. He'd learned all of that from the little card tucked within the arrangement. "These are for you."

He didn't know it was possible, but her smile broadened. She accepted the bouquet and sniffed the blooms. "Thank you. They're beautiful!"

It was on the tip of his tongue to tell her that their beauty paled in comparison to hers, but he bit back the words. He couldn't read more into this meal than she intended. This was a friendly gesture. Nothing more.

And then as though she realized he was still standing outside, she opened the door wide. "Come on in."

When he stepped past her, he inhaled the lightest scent. His eyes momentarily drifted closed as he appreciated her perfume. He couldn't name it, but it had a hint of citrus mixed with floral. He wanted to pause so he could breathe in deeper.

Instead, he kept walking. But he didn't get far before the kitten ran up to him. The kitten pranced about, meowing. A smile pulled at his lips. He'd never had anyone so excited to see him. He couldn't help but wonder if this was what Sara came home to each day.

He knelt down and picked up the kitten. "And how are you?"

"Meow. Meow. Meow."

"Really?" His smile broadened as the kitten continued to talk to him. "You're a chatty one."

"He likes you."

Kent held the kitten against his chest as he continued to pet him. "You think so?"

She nodded. "But don't get too attached. He'll be going home any day now."

"Do you still believe that?"

"Sure. Why wouldn't I?"

He petted the kitten's head. "I don't know. You two seem happy together. I thought maybe you'd want to go take down the flyers and keep him."

A smile lifted Sara's lips and puffed up her cheeks. "We are getting used to each other." Her gaze moved to the kitten. "Aren't we?"

Sara stepped up to them and reached out to the pet the kitten. "Maybe you're right. After all, if someone was going to claim him, they'd have done it by now."

"I totally agree." He took in the sight of Sara looking lovingly at the kitten. "So it's official. You two are now a family."

Instead of smiling at his comment, Sara frowned. Her eyes shimmered with unshed tears. *Oh no.* What had he said wrong?

He gently set the kitten on the floor and then turned to Sara. "What's the matter? What did I say wrong?"

She swiped at her eyes and then she smiled at him. "You didn't say anything wrong."

"I don't understand. You look like I upset you."

"You didn't. I promise. It's just been so long since I had family around me. And now I have the kitten. He is so sweet and insists on sleeping on my pillow every night. And Cari is coming home. This is going to be the best summer ever."

He released a pent-up breath. "I'm so glad it's all working out for you. I hope this summer all of your dreams come true."

"They will." There was a distinct note of confidence in her voice. "Now let's get some food."

"Wait. I have one more gift." He reached into his pocket and pulled out a pack of catnip mice.

"Aww... That's so sweet." Her tears were replaced with a big smile. "The kitten will love them."

Kent opened the package and placed a little white mouse on the floor in front of the kitten. At first the kitten wasn't sure what to make of it. But after a sniff and a tentative pawing, the kitty set about batting the mouse around the living room.

"I think he approves." Kent continued to watch the kitten as it got too rambunctious and fell over.

"I think you're right. Now let's eat."

As Kent followed her to the kitchen, he told himself not to let himself enjoy this evening too much. It wasn't like it was going to lead anywhere. Even if the past was finally left in the past, he wouldn't let the evening get out of hand. It was best for both of them.

Dinner was only okay.

But the company was excellent.

Sara sat on her deck with Kent next to her. The sun hovered low in the horizon. Its last rays of gold splashed over the ocean. It was a beautiful sight and one she would never tire of seeing.

But it was his company she'd enjoyed the most. They'd kept their conversation centered around the inn, as though each of them was worried about treading into personal territory.

She knew why he was holding back. It was her fault. She'd jumped to the wrong conclusion about him years ago, and it had left an awkwardness between them. They'd worked hard to overcome it, but it wouldn't be fully resolved until she spoke up and fixed things.

"You really didn't have to do all of this." Kent's voice interrupted her thoughts.

She blinked and looked at him. It took a moment for his words to register in her mind. And then she realized that she'd forgotten something. "I forgot dessert. I'll be right back."

"You don't have to bother."

She ignored him and rushed into her kitchen. She didn't keep a lot of sweets on hand because if she did, she'd eat them, and she didn't need the extra calories.

She opened the fridge to see if there was something to offer him. There wasn't. She shut the door and then started opening and closing the cabinets. Above the stove she found an unopened package of chocolate sandwich cookies. She wondered how long they'd been up there. She checked the expiration date and found that they were still good.

She rushed back to the deck. She sat down and held the cookies out to him. "These are all I have. Hope you like them."

He smiled and took a couple. "Thanks."

"You're just lucky that I put them in the cabinet and forgot about them because I love them." She took a cookie and munched on it.

Sara just hoped Kent would accept her heartfelt apology, and they could form a closer relationship. She wanted to be able to talk to him about so much more than the refresh project and the beautiful summer weather. But once she peeled back the wounds from the past, would they be able to heal?

Before she changed her mind, she said, "I need to apologize to you."

The smile slipped from Kent's face. "You have nothing to apologize for. Your cooking was excellent."

"I'm not talking about dinner."

He sighed. "I didn't think you were, but I was just hoping—"

"That I wasn't going to apologize to you?"

He shrugged. "It's not necessary. All of that is in the past." He looked at her with an arched brow. "Did you talk to Cari?"

She nodded. "She told me everything. I just wished you had been the one who had told me."

"I told you—"

"I know. It wasn't your secret." She turned her deck chair to face him. "And you thought it was a good idea to let me go on hating you instead of telling me that you were a hero."

His face filled with color. She didn't think she'd ever seen him embarrassed before. It was such a cute look on him.

He glanced down. "I just did what anyone else would do."

"No." She shook her head. "You went above and beyond for her. And instead of me being eternally indebted to you, I was a jerk. I'm so sorry. I never should have said those things to you or accused you of being a jerk. Please forgive me."

"It's like I said before, there's nothing to forgive."

"Yes, there is."

His gaze rose and met hers. "No, because you were just being a protective sister. There was no way for you to know what had happened with your sister that summer. It's the way she wanted it. It was the only way I could convince her to go get professional help."

Sara leaned forward and pressed her hand to his forearm, feeling his corded muscles beneath her fingertips. "Thank you for being there for Cari. I wish she'd felt she could turn to me, but I'm glad she had you."

"She was protecting you." He reached out, catching her hand within his own. "You have to know that she was more concerned about you than herself. She was worried after the death of your father that you couldn't take anymore."

The unexpected death of her father had sent her into a tailspin. For a time, she wasn't even sure she was going to bother finishing college. Her family had meant everything to her. When she was young, they'd spent a lot of quality time together, playing board games on Sunday evenings, going fishing in her father's old boat, and a million other little things that wove them together.

When her mother had died, the threads of her family started to unravel. Their time together faded away and her father had gotten lost in his grief. When at last her father started to find his way back to them, he had a fatal heart attack.

At that point, Sara had felt herself getting swept up in a tsunami of grief. The current was so strong she'd felt herself getting pulled away from the person she'd once been. In order to feel something besides the constant pain, she'd acted out. She'd done things that were dangerous because she figured it didn't matter if she lived or died. She'd lost her anchor.

The only thing that had pulled her back from the edge was her sister. Cari had stepped up and yelled in Sara's face when she needed a wake-up call. Sara didn't know what she'd have done without sister.

It made Sara sad that she'd been so caught up in her own stuff that she couldn't be there for her sister. When Cari finally returned to Bluestar, Sara wouldn't make the same mistake. She would make room for Cari in her life. She would be there for her. And maybe now that they were both grown up, they could become the best friends she'd always thought they'd been.

"Are you okay?" Kent's deep voice was laced with concern.

She blinked repeatedly and nodded. "I'm good." Her gaze lifted and met his. "How about us? Are we good?"

"We are. And now I should help you clean up the dishes before I leave so you can get some rest before you have to go to work in the morning."

They both went to stand at the same time and bumped into each other. Her heart skipped a beat. She should pull back, but she didn't want to.

As a teenager, she'd wondered what it would be like to be kissed by Kent. When she'd thought her sister was dating him, jealousy had burned within her. She'd done everything she could to ignore the reaction. She'd told herself that Kent was off-limits forevermore. Who knew that she'd been utterly and completely wrong?

Her heart beat so loudly now it echoed in her ears. She noticed he didn't move either. Did he hear her heart? Did he know she longed to feel his lips pressed to hers?

For so long she'd been fighting her feelings for him because of her sister, but now she had her sister's blessing to act on those feelings. But did Kent feel the same way? Did he want to feel her lips pressed to his?

She lifted her gaze until it met his. He stared deeply into her eyes. There was desire reflected in them. No one had ever looked at her that way before. She thought her heart was going to pound its way out of her chest.

She wanted to reach up and pull his head down to her, but her body refused to cooperate. It was as though a spell had been cast over her. She stood there with her pulse racing while waiting and wondering what Kent was going to do.

She willed him to kiss her. She'd never wanted anything more in her life. Every cell in her body longed to feel his touch—to feel his strong arms wrapped around her as his lips moved over hers.

And then he lowered his head toward her. Her eyelids fluttered shut. His lips pressed to hers. She couldn't believe this was happening. It was something she'd wanted so badly when she'd been a teenager and then again when they started working on the inn, but she never thought it would be possible.

If this was a dream, she never wanted to wake up. Because his kiss was so much better than anything she'd ever imagined.

The sound of a dog barking on the beach had Kent pulling back. "I'm sorry. I shouldn't have done that."

She opened her mouth to disagree with him but then silently pressed her lips together. What was she supposed to say? That she vehemently disagreed with him? That if the horribleness hadn't happened with her sister they might have gotten together long before this?

None of that seemed to matter if he didn't feel the same way about her. And yet there was nothing in his kiss that said he hadn't enjoyed it too. Maybe there was another reason he'd pulled away.

"I'll get these dishes to the kitchen." He scooped up their now-empty coffee mugs and headed inside her apartment.

She stood there alone on the deck for a moment, gathering her thoughts. How was she supposed to go in there and act as though nothing had happened? She didn't know if she was that good of an actor.

She drew in a deep breath, hoping it would calm her racing heart. She held it for a moment and then slowly blew it out. She repeated the process. And then she walked inside, hoping when she spoke that her voice didn't betray the most unsettled feelings he'd evoked in her.

When she found him standing at the sink with a soapy cloth in hand as he washed one of the dinner dishes, she was touched. She'd never had a date where the guy hung around to do the dishes. She thought of telling him that she had a dishwasher discreetly tucked away behind the cabinetry, but she didn't want to do anything that might upset him.

And so she picked up a drying towel and set to work drying the dishes and returning them to their proper spot. It was all very domesticated, except for the part where they weren't speaking to each other.

When the last dish was washed, dried, and put away, he turned to her. "Thank you for dinner. It was the best I've had in a long time."

"You're welcome."

He turned and found the kitten sitting there. "Goodnight." He paused and glanced over at her. "What are you going to call him? You can't keep calling him kitty."

"I...I don't know." She had been procrastinating. She'd been thinking that the cat's family would have come for him by now. But with each passing day that was becoming less likely. "What do you think I should call him?"

"Shadow?"

She shook her head.

"Blackie?"

She shook her head again.

Kent was quiet for a moment, as though giving the idea some serious thought. His gaze moved around the room, as though he were searching for an idea. Then his eyes widened as a smile lifted the corners of his lips. "I know."

"Are you going to share?" She was really curious to hear his idea.

"Oreo."

"Oreo?" She rolled the name around in her mind.

"Sure. You love the cookies, and you love the kitty. So it makes sense."

She wanted to argue with his logic, but she couldn't. She looked at Oreo. With his black and white features, the name fit. "Oreo it is."

"Did you hear that, Oreo? You now have a name." Kent fussed over the cat before turning to her. "I really do need to go. It's getting late. Thank you for everything."

"You're welcome."

He turned for the door. She knew by the quickness of his steps that it was too much to hope for a kiss goodnight. She followed him to the doorway. When he paused and looked back at her, she uttered, "Yes, you should have."

He sent her a puzzled look. She regretted her spontaneous utterance. What had she been thinking?

The truth was she hadn't been thinking; she'd been acting on her heightened emotions—a hangover from their kiss.

His eyes widened. His brows rose. It was as though he finally realized she'd been referring to the kiss. Her heart pounded as she waited for his reaction. Had her admission been a mistake?

Her body tensed as time felt as though it were suspended. Part of her wanted to go back and never issue the dinner invitation. And the other part didn't regret a single moment of their evening together. But as things stood, it came down to how Kent felt about them—about the kiss.

And then a smile lifted the corners of his lips. It was a slight smile at first, but then it grew. It eased the stress lines on his face and made him look irresistibly handsome.

"Goodnight." He leaned toward her.

Her heart launched into her throat. She didn't move. She was unsure what he was going to do.

Her eyes closed as the anticipation rose. And then his lips touched her cheek. Before she could respond in any way, he pulled away. The kiss was so brief and a whisper of a touch that she had to wonder if she'd imagined it.

Without another word, he turned and headed down the steps. She stood on the landing, watching as he faded away into the shadows of the night. A dreamy sigh escaped her lips as her fingers pressed to her cheek where his lips had just been a few moments ago.

To say she was confused was an understatement. She had no idea where this left them. She had a feeling she wouldn't get much sleep that night.

Chapter Thirteen

W HAT HAD HE BEEN thinking?

It was the question Kent had asked himself the rest of the night and into the next day. Not able to sleep, he'd trolled the internet searching for a job that would take him away from Bluestar Island. He didn't have any right to get involved with Sara.

Sometime in the twilight hours, he'd come to the conclusion that if he stopped this thing with Sara—whatever you wanted to call it—then there would be no harm, no foul. It was a spontaneous kiss after a lovely dinner.

Surely Sara could understand that, especially if it didn't happen again. They would remain friends—nothing more.

After getting a few hours of restless sleep, he was up extra early. He'd checked his computer and dealt with his emails. So far he'd had two thanks-but-no-thanks responses to his applications for various financial positions in Boston.

Intent on not letting his life go back to the same routine he had at the furniture store, he searched outside of Boston until he found two more potential positions, and then he applied. That made a total of five applications he had out in the world. Surely he'd hear a positive response from at least one of them.

In the meantime, he had to hold Sara at arm's length. He knew it wouldn't be easy—perhaps not for either one of them. But the last thing he wanted to do was hurt her. With some time before the furniture was to be delivered, he formulated a plan—something to help Sara. When he arrived at the inn mid-morning—much later than he normally started working—he didn't go straight to the lobby. Instead, he went in search of Sara, who was just finishing speaking with some guests.

When her gaze landed on him, her whole face lit up. He basked in her sunny glow. It made his heart beat quickly. He chose to ignore the reason for his reaction.

He made his way to her. "Good morning."

"Good morning to you too. Are you just getting here?"

"As a matter of fact, I am." He chose not to expand upon his reason for starting work late. "Can you take a break?"

"I, uh..." She glanced down at the digital notebook in her hand. She tapped on the screen, bringing it to life. After a quick glance, she looked up at him. "I have a little time. What do you have in mind?"

"Come with me."

Her eyes widened. "Where are we going? I can't just disappear."

"But you do get a break, don't you?"

"Yes." She still looked hesitantly at him.

"Then let someone know you'll be gone for a few minutes."

For a moment, she didn't move. He was starting to think she was going to refuse him. Then she reached for her phone and sent a text message.

"Since you don't have much time, I think we'll take my cart. Come on." He set off toward the parking area.

"But you still haven't told me where we're going."

"That's true." He subdued a smile and kept walking. Once they were both seated in the cart, he started it. "I thought you could use a coffee break."

A smile lifted the corners of her mouth. "I think that sounds like a good idea."

He failed to mention that he had a few stops along the way, but he liked that she'd trusted him and come with him without knowing where they were going. It said a lot about their relationship and how it had blossomed that summer. Not only was the inn getting a refresh, but so was their relationship. He just hoped when he moved away for work that it wouldn't ruin the friendship they'd built. He'd like to think when he returned to the island they could still grab some coffee and catch up with each other.

He was up to something.

Of that she was certain. But what?

Sara sat in the passenger seat of his cart as they headed into the heart of Bluestar. When he suddenly pulled to a stop, she glanced around. What was he doing? No one sold coffee here.

Kent got out of the cart, and she followed his lead. When he looked at her, she sent him a what-are-you-doing look.

His smile broadened, making her heart skip a beat. He was so incredibly handsome, but when he smiled, he was even more dashing. And yet she had no idea where their relationship stood. Because when he'd gone to leave the night before, he hadn't clarified anything with that kiss on the cheek. Did it mean he wanted to see where things were headed? Or was it his way of politely rejecting her?

She wanted to ask him, but every time she went to say something, the words would clog the back of her throat. Now she was left with trying to read something into his actions. It wasn't helping. All she was doing was confusing herself even further.

He stepped up onto the sidewalk. She thought he was approaching her, but instead he moved to a utility pole and removed a piece of paper from it. It took her a moment to realize the paper was the found kitten notice they'd posted around town for Oreo.

A smile pulled at her lips, but she resisted giving into it. "What are you doing?"

"Removing the notices for Oreo." His gaze met hers. "After all, he's no longer lost. He's home now, right?"

It had been a week now since she'd taken in the kitten. It was a small town. If someone was going to claim her, they would have done it by now.

Sara smiled and nodded. "Oreo is most definitely home."

"Good. We have a lot of flyers to collect."

And so they took down the flyers as quickly as possible. Sara liked the thought of no longer being all alone. There was just something so comforting about coming home to the tiny fluff ball whose purr made his entire body vibrate.

Oreo needed a home. And Sara needed a family. It appeared they'd come into each other's lives at just the right time.

———ele———

His back ached and his knees throbbed.

Kent slowly got to his feet. He would never let anyone convince him that laying flooring was easy. It didn't matter what type of flooring it was—vinyl, tile, or wood—working on your knees wasn't for wimps.

He hoped when his sister returned at the end of the week that she would appreciate all of the hard work. As he stretched out the kinks in his muscles from being hunched over putting in the last pieces of flooring, he glanced around at all the progress they'd made.

The lobby was almost finished. They just had to put back all the pieces—there were a lot of them. Earlier that day the new furniture had been delivered. It was sitting across the room from where he was standing. The pieces were still wrapped in plastic to keep them clean.

Speaking of keeping things clean, he needed to clean up this place before they could move on to the final step of setting the stage or, in this case, the room. He set to work vacuuming and mopping.

As he cleaned, he found a couple of places where the paint needed touching up. He was really pleased with how the project was turning out. He hoped Josie would think the same thing.

He was moving the various pieces into place when he heard someone behind him. He finished moving a display case into place and then turned. There stood Sara with her arms crossed as she took in the room.

How was it possible that she grew more beautiful each time he saw her? Her short hair was tucked behind one of her ears. Her trio of diamond stud earrings glittered in the light.

He noticed she didn't wear a lot of makeup. She didn't need it. Her complexion was unblemished, and her dark lashes outlined her eyes.

Not so long ago, he'd held her in his arms and pressed his lips to hers. He longed to go to her and do it again, but he didn't allow himself that luxury. He couldn't let himself get wrapped up in her. If he did, he'd never get out of the rut his life was in. But he couldn't deny that it was tempting—oh so tempting.

He swallowed hard. "What do you think?"

"I can't believe it's almost finished."

He smiled. "I'm glad I was able to surprise you in a good way."

"What else are you planning to do?"

"I don't know. Put back all of the historical stuff and then place the new furniture."

She turned her head as she took in the room that looked so much larger with the lighter colors. "We should put up some new curtains."

"Curtains?" He glanced at the large windows that looked out over the covered porch. "Really?"

"Sure. After all, with the new floor and fresh paint on the walls, you don't want to hang the same old drab curtains."

She did have a point. How much work can hanging curtains be? "Okay."

Sara walked over to the doorway and stared into the room, as though she were mulling over another change. "We'll also need a throw rug and a runner from the door to the registration desk."

Kent rubbed the back of his neck. The runner was already taken care of. However, finding matching throw rugs would require a special order. He hadn't thought about all of these details. "I don't know."

"Oh, come on. You want this place to look its best, don't you?"

He hated that she had another good point. "Okay. We'll get a couple of throw rugs to go with the runner. But that's all."

She frowned at him. "Why are you being like that?"

"Being like what?"

"Stubborn." She crossed her arms and frowned at him. "I'm just trying to help you."

He sighed. "What else did you have in mind?"

She eyed him up, as though to decide if he was serious or not. As the silence stretched on, he realized she needed more prompting.

"I'm serious," he said. "Just tell me your thoughts. The other ideas weren't so bad."

"Not so bad?" A slight smile lifted the corners of her lips. "As in they were good ideas?"

Her eyes prodded him for confirmation. He could sense she wasn't going to give in. "Yes, they are good ideas."

She arched a brow. "Just good ideas?"

He inwardly groaned. What was up with her? He'd never known her to push so hard for a compliment. "Okay. They're great ideas."

Her smile broadened. "There. That wasn't so hard, was it?"

He rolled his eyes. "Now what is your other idea?"

"I think we should dress the place up with fresh plants, and on the coffee tables we should place some of those big colorful books filled with beautiful pictures."

He honestly hadn't thought of any of this stuff. "It sounds a little over the top. Don't we want to save some of this stuff for Josie?"

Sara shook her head. "Josie has a lot going on. We should have this place totally setup and ready to go when she gets home."

He opened his mouth to argue the point further, but then he saw the determined look on Sara's face. She wasn't going to give up until the lobby was completed. He wordlessly pressed his lips together.

"So you agree." She stated it as a matter of fact. "Good. Tomorrow let's go shopping."

He was afraid she'd say that. Shopping wasn't one of his favorite tasks. But with Sara by his side, it certainly would be interesting, especially when she looked at him with that bright sunny smile that made his heart skip a beat.

Chapter Fourteen

IT HAD BEEN A fun afternoon of shopping.

Even Kent had smiled a time or two.

Friday afternoon, Sara insisted on driving one of the inn's carts. It was larger than Kent's and would provide more room for the plants and decorations they picked up along the way.

She'd be the first to admit that she was opposed to this refresh project, but now that it was almost complete, she loved it. The lobby looked like a totally different place. It was so much more welcoming. She couldn't wait for Josie to see it.

She glanced over at Kent to say something and noticed him staring at his phone...again. He'd been doing that a lot today. She wondered what had him so distracted.

"Is everything okay?" She slowed the cart to a stop at a busy intersection.

"You mean other than being dragged along on this shopping trip?" He sent her a teasing smile.

"Oh. You love it. And you know it."

He let out a laugh. "Is that what you really think?"

"Of course. You're with me. Why wouldn't you have a good time?"

He continued to smile and shake his head. "Think highly of yourself much?"

The smile fell from her face. Is that what he really thought of her? That she was stuck up? She was only trying to have a little bit of fun. "That isn't what I meant. I was just having some fun."

"Hey. Relax," Kent said. "I was just giving you a hard time."

Her gaze searched his. "Do you mean it? You're not just saying it to make me feel better, are you?"

"Of course not." He frowned. "I meant that in response to your first question. And yes, I meant it." His phone buzzed, drawing his attention.

"What's going on with you?"

He stared at his phone but didn't answer it. "Nothing. Why?"

"Because you've been distracted with your phone all afternoon."

He shrugged. "I just have some stuff going on."

"Oh." She wanted to ask more but she didn't.

An awkward silence ensued before he said, "I've gotten an interview for a job in Boston."

"That's great news." She put on her best and brightest smile, even though on the inside she hoped he wouldn't leave Bluestar.

He returned her smile, but she noticed it didn't light up his eyes. "There's no guarantee about a job, but it's at least a start."

"When is the interview?"

"Next week. So we've got to get these last details at the inn completed before then."

"It shouldn't be a problem. We just need to take care of the details." She pulled the cart to a stop. "We're here."

They both got out of the cart and stared up at the Seaside Bookshop. She loved this little shop. Of course, it didn't hurt that the owner, Melinda Coleman, was a good friend. She was also Harvey's daughter.

Melinda had been by her side through the death of both of Sara's parents as well as Cari moving away. Sara didn't know how she'd have gotten through any of it without her. Melinda did more listening than she did talking. She let Sara get all of the pain out in the open. And then there were other times when talking wasn't needed, and they'd sit together watching a movie. Sometimes Sara watched the television and other times she let her thoughts meander as she came to terms with the changes in her life.

Sara hadn't told Melinda they were stopping by today. Frankly, she hadn't been so certain Kent would go along with her idea. He seemed like he was ready to be done with this project once and for all.

She couldn't blame him. They'd been working on the lobby for a week now. And this was supposed to be Kent's vacation. She felt bad that he'd spent so much of it working.

At least the refresh project was coming to an end. Hopefully he'd get some time to relax before he had to go back to work. He deserved it after all of the hard work he'd done for his sister.

And then she realized that at the end of next week was the Concert on the Beach, and they had a date. Not an official date but plans for the evening. Her stomach fluttered at the thought of spending more time with Kent.

As they both got out of the cart and headed toward the bookshop, she said, "I'm sorry you haven't been able to enjoy your vacation."

"Don't be. This was all my idea. The refresh project helped me figure something out."

"What's that?"

"I don't want to do refresh projects every day. It was more involved than I'd been thinking." He glanced at her. "And I appreciate all of your help. I'm sorry it's taken up so much of your time."

"It's okay. It was for a good cause. Besides, I have some vacation time saved up too. After this week of working from morning until night, I'm thinking I might take some time off after Josie returns to relax with Oreo and maybe read a book at the beach with my toes in the sand."

"Sounds nice. Maybe I should join you."

Her heart leapt into her throat. Was he serious? She swallowed hard and hoped that when she spoke, her voice sounded normal. "You definitely should."

He hesitated as though he was trying to figure out if she was serious or not. "I don't know. After all, Oreo needs someone to play with while you're sunbathing."

She arched a brow. "You think my kitten likes you that much?"

"Actually, I think he does."

It wasn't just the kitten that liked Kent a lot. When she glanced at him and his gaze met hers, her heart thump-thumped as heat rushed to her cheeks. Not that she was going to act on her feelings. She glanced away. After all, he was planning to move.

It didn't go unnoticed by Kent that Sara was now calling Oreo "my kitten." He was glad Sara had found the kitten. She seemed to need Oreo in her life.

He didn't get a chance to say more as they reached the bookshop. It was a charming older brick building that had been whitewashed. The display window had a display that included a pink, blue, and yellow striped beach towel, sunglasses, a fruity drink, and books. Lots of books. And then he noticed a stuffed dog with a corner of the towel in its mouth, as though it were pulling it. Kent couldn't help but smile. Whoever created the display had a lot of imagination.

The Seaside Bookshop was owned and operated by Melinda Coleman. He knew her from town hall meetings and other events around town. She was one of those friendly people that were easy to talk to.

He pulled the wooden door with a large glass window open. The brass bell above the door jingled. The air conditioning was most welcome on such a warm day.

The bookshop was busy with both young and old people meandering up and down the aisles. He'd only been in the shop a couple of times. Reading wasn't one of his hobbies. He supposed that was because he spent a lot of his free time playing softball with his brothers or going fishing out on the ocean.

To both the left and right were bookshelves crammed full of books. Directly in front of them was the checkout counter. No one was tending it. They must be helping one of the customers.

He'd never seen so many books in one place. The signs at the end of the aisles indicated they had books on most every subject. Maybe he should pick out one or two books and join Sara on the beach. The offer was certainly tempting.

His gaze moved to Sara, who was glancing around the shop. He'd really enjoyed getting to know her. She was so different than he'd originally thought. He'd assumed that she carried grudges, but once she learned her sister's secret, she'd let go of the past.

"Kent?" Sara waved a hand in front of his face. "Didn't you hear me?"

He blinked. "Uh, sorry. What did you say?"

She frowned at him. "What's wrong with you?"

"Nothing." Things had gotten awkward after their kiss. He couldn't make them even more complicated.

Her gaze searched his. "You sure?"

"Positive."

"Hey, Sara. I thought I saw you walk in." Melinda approached them with a smile on her face. Her gaze moved between the two of them. "Are you two together?"

Immediately, he shook his head.

They both said in unison, "No."

"Oh. I'm sorry." Melinda looked a bit flushed. "My mistake."

"We're not *together* together," Sara clarified. "But we're here together to pick out some coffee table books for the inn's lobby."

Melinda's eyes widened. "Is this for the lobby remodel? I heard it was going on while Josie was out of town."

"It's not a remodel," Kent said.

"It's a refresh." Sara reached into her purse and pulled out her phone. Her fingers moved rapidly over the screen. "Here are some photos, but they don't really do the room justice."

Melinda took the phone and scrolled through the photos that Kent didn't even know existed. It was a good idea. He should do that when they got back to the inn.

"This looks fantastic." Melinda continued to stare at the images. "I'd like to get something like that done here."

Her statement drew Kent's interest. If he could keep drumming up business, maybe he could hire some help, and then the refresh project wouldn't seem so overwhelming. As soon as the thought came to him, he dismissed it. He'd already investigated going out on his own, and he knew the statistics weren't in favor of a new business. His best option was to take an accounting position in a big company.

Still, it wouldn't hurt to hear what Melinda had to say. "What did you have in mind?"

She gestured to the bookshelves in front of the display window. "I was thinking of doing away with these bookshelves and making room for a reading nook. This window lets in a lot of light, and I thought some people might want to hang out and read. I could even offer some refreshments. What better advertisement could a bookstore have than a bunch of people reading?"

"Oh, I like the idea," Sara said. "What would you do? Add a couple of couches and chairs?"

Melinda shook her head. "I want something unique. Like different shaped benches with little tables for drinks." She gestured to the ceiling. "With the very high ceilings in here, I even wondered if it would be possible to put in a loft."

"I love the sound of it," Sara said. "You might even put in some seating for the little kids."

"That's a great idea." Melinda's eyes lit up. She turned to him. "Can you do something like that?"

"It's way outside of my capabilities. But my brother Liam makes handcrafted furniture. He might be able to come up with some stuff for you." He reached for his wallet and withdrew a business card with his brother's information. "You can reach him here. But I have to warn you that he's in high demand, and he has custody of his little boy this summer, so it might be a while until he's able to work on it."

Melinda took the card. "Thanks. The inn's lobby really does look amazing. You two do good work."

"It was Kent's idea," Sara said. "I wasn't so sure about it, but he did what needed to be done in order to give the place a polished look, which is what brought us here."

"And now you just need the finishing touches?" Melinda's gaze moved between them.

Sara nodded. "We were thinking about some big, colorful books."

"Oh sure." Melinda started to move toward the back of the shop. "Do you have a particular subject in mind?"

Sara sent him a questioning look. This was her idea. Why was she looking at him? She raised her brows as though prompting him to say something.

He said the first thing that came to mind. "How about something that has to do with the ocean?"

It wasn't exactly creative, but considering the Brass Anchor Inn was situated on the beach, it made sense. And hopefully it would tie in with all of the Bluestar Island memorabilia.

Sara nodded. "It sounds good to me."

Buzz.

It was his phone. He pulled it from his back pocket and saw the name of one of the companies that he'd applied to. "I've got to take this."

"Go ahead," Sara said. "We've got this."

He pressed the phone to his ear as he turned for the door. This was one of the calls he'd been waiting for—hoping for. But now that they'd called, he didn't feel the elation he'd been expecting.

CHAPTER FIFTEEN

S HE COULDN'T WAIT.

Monday afternoon, Sara couldn't stop smiling. It wouldn't be long now until she saw her sister. It'd been close to two years since they'd last been in the same place at the same time. And now everything was coming together.

At the end of the month, Cari would be back on Bluestar Island. Sara's family would at last be whole once more. She couldn't wait to introduce Cari to the newest member of the family, Oreo.

"What are you smiling about?" Kent's voice drew her from her thoughts.

Sara glanced across the lobby at him. "I was just thinking that Cari will be home soon."

He approached her. "Speaking of your sister, I haven't received a signed lease or a deposit."

"That's strange." Cari recalled how hard it was to get ahold of her sister—even harder than before she started the process to move home. "She's been really busy lately with the move and everything."

"I understand. But we also have other people interested in the apartment. I just need to know she's serious about the place."

"She is!" The words came out quicker and more emphatic than she'd intended.

"You're really excited about her coming home, aren't you?" He studied her.

She nodded. There was absolutely no point in denying it. "She's the only family I have left. We were close when we were younger. I hope we can be that way again."

"Don't forget that she's been gone for years. She might have changed."

Sara shook her head. "I talk to her. Cari is still the sister I used to know."

"Maybe she is. I just know with my siblings that we've all grown and changed. Look at Liam. He's now a father. I still can't believe my little brother has a son of his own. And he's such a good parent."

She didn't know Liam very well. He was several years ahead of her in school, and they didn't share the same group of friends. He seemed like a nice guy and was handsome but not nearly as good-looking as Kent.

"I saw him with his little boy in town a while back. They looked really cute together. It's a shame his marriage didn't work out."

"They tried to make it work, but they wanted different things. Eventually, it pulled them apart."

She wondered if that was what would happen if she and Kent were to get together. Would he eventually resent her for keeping him on the island instead of letting him follow his dreams to the mainland? She couldn't imagine the pain of falling in love with someone and expecting to be together forever, and then one day it's over. The pain must be staggering. And something she didn't want to put herself or Kent through.

It was better for her to concentrate on things she could control—like making her sister's homecoming the best it could be. She wanted her sister to know how much she'd missed her and how welcome she was in Bluestar. Maybe she should plan a welcome home party, but first she needed to know when her sister's arrival would be.

And then she had another moment of genius. "I know. We should do a refresh project on my sister's apartment."

"Whoa. You're jumping ahead."

She sent him a puzzled look. "You don't want to fix up the place?"

"It's not that. She hasn't committed to taking the apartment."

"I'm sorry. She's been super busy. She's been gone a really long time. She must have collected a lot of stuff." Sara wasn't about to let this apartment slip through their fingers. "I can put down a deposit and sign the lease."

He shook his head. "You don't have to do that."

"I know I don't, but I want to. Cari needs the place. Don't worry. She'll pay me back when she gets home." She trusted her sister. They used to be so close. She wanted to regain that closeness once more.

Kent picked up a rolled-up throw rug and slung it over his shoulder. "You don't have to do that. You said she'll be home by the end of the month, right?" When she nodded, he said, "We can wait until then."

"Really?"

When he nodded, she rushed to him. It wasn't until she was there with her arms wrapped around him and his body stiff that she realized she'd overstepped. They'd been tiptoeing around this thing between them. And it was obvious Kent wasn't ready to take things any further than that one kiss.

Just as she was about to pull away, his free arm wrapped around her, pulling her closer. Her heart pitter-pattered. Maybe he did feel something for her.

When his arm fell away, she grudgingly backed away. His gaze met hers and held long enough for her pulse to hit triple digits. His gaze dipped to her lips. With all of her might, she willed him to kiss her.

In that moment, she didn't think about all of the reasons it was a bad idea. Time seemed to be suspended as they gazed at each other. Perhaps she should make the first move. Maybe he wasn't sure how she felt about him. Though how could that be? She felt as though her emotions were evident on her face.

His gaze fell away, breaking the moment. Disappointment engulfed her as an awkward silence ensued. She should say something—anything—but her mouth wouldn't work. Kent turned away and moved the rug into place.

❧

He'd almost kissed her.

What had he been thinking?

The next day, Kent had a hard time concentrating. He kept thinking about how close he'd come to pulling Sara close and pressing his lips to hers. Even though he'd reminded himself of all the reasons he needed to keep his distance, it didn't make him want to kiss her any less.

There was something about Sara that had him wanting things he knew should be off limits. After all, he was in the process of making plans to leave the island in the near future. It would be wrong to start anything at this point.

Maybe that was why he was so tempted—because he knew nothing serious could come of it. He wouldn't have to worry about strings and commitments. The only thing holding him back was the fact he wouldn't intentionally do anything to hurt Sara. And that was why he would keep a respectable distance between them.

His thoughts were interrupted when Birdie Neill and Agnes Dewey stopped by to check out the updates to the lobby. Birdie was full of compliments while Agnes was quiet and only spoke up when she found a small flaw. Birdie promised to spread the word around town about the amazing job he'd done. He wondered if it would generate much interest among the islanders.

The lobby would be completed today. It would have been finished yesterday but Sara had come up with an idea for some additional trim work on the walls to highlight the framed photos.

The trim work wasn't hard. It just took time because the carved pieces of wood had to be painted white, making sure not to miss any of the crevices. And then Sara thought some gold highlights would give the trim a more impressive look.

He didn't think it needed the gold paint. The truth was that he didn't want to take the time. The more time he spent with Sara, the more confused he became about his future.

That morning he'd had his second video interview. It had gone well. At least he thought it had gone well. And he'd heard back on a phone interview that he'd done at the beginning of the week. They asked him to come in for an in-person interview.

He was pumped about the position. It was the right salary, and the position sounded interesting. The only catch was that he had to work in Hartford, Connecticut. That was a bit farther from Bluestar than he'd hoped. But he was getting ahead of himself. He didn't even have the job yet.

He'd been outside, cutting one of the painted pieces of trim. It was a half an inch too long. When he stepped into the lobby, he saw Sara on her phone. She wasn't saying anything, but the frown on her face was quite evident.

When she slipped the phone into her pocket, he asked, "Is everything all right?"

She nodded. "I was trying to reach Cari. With the time difference, it's hard to get a hold of each other. I just wanted to see if she'd gotten the lease signed and to find out when she's flying in. I can't believe she'll be here in just a couple of weeks."

He could hear the excitement in her voice. He was happy for Sara. She'd be so busy catching up on things with her sister that she wouldn't notice when he moved away. At least that was what he told himself to feel better about his plans. After all, it wasn't like they were in a relationship or anything.

Knock-knock.

He glanced to the doorway to find a middle-aged couple standing there. He approached them. "Sorry. The lobby is under renovations right now. If you go down one door, it'll lead you to the temporary check-in desk."

"Oh. We're not here to check in," the woman with a short brown bob haircut said. Her gaze moved to Sara. "We're here to see her."

"Me?" Sara pressed a hand to her chest as her eyes momentarily widened. It appeared she hadn't been expecting them. "I'm Sara Chen. What can I do for you?"

The woman glanced down at the protective covering on the floor. "Can we step inside?"

"Sure." Sara stepped forward. Kent decided to follow just to make sure everything was okay.

"I'm Maude Watson and my husband's name is Charles. It's nice to meet you."

When their gazes moved to Kent, he said, "I'm Kent Turner. Sara and I are business partners."

"I see." The woman's gaze flickered between the two of them. "We tried your apartment first, but obviously you weren't there. And then Birdie was out with her dog, and when she heard that we needed to speak with you, she guided us here." The middle-aged woman wrung her hands together as her words ran one into another.

"What my wife is trying to say is that the kitten you found is ours," the husband said.

"Yours?" The emphasis on the one-word response didn't go unnoticed by any of them.

"Yes." Maude's response was immediate.

"You see," Charles said, "we were on vacation—visiting with family—and we had the teenager from next door stop by a couple of times a day to feed the cats. He didn't notice that one had gone missing. He claims it didn't get out when he was there."

"How would he know?" Maude frowned. "He didn't even look for the cats. He just dropped some food and changed the water."

As the couple continued to explain about the lost kitten, Kent glanced at Sara. The smile that had been on her face all day as they worked on the final touches to the lobby had faded away. In its place were frown lines as pain shone in her eyes. Guilt heaped onto his shoulders. He'd played a part in Sara bonding with Oreo. After so long, he never thought anyone would come to claim the kitten.

"Let me grab my keys, and I'll take you to get, um, the kitten." When Sara turned around, she averted her gaze from him.

He walked with her to the other end of the lobby where they kept their personal items. "I'm so sorry about this."

She shook off his apology. "It's not your fault."

"Yes, it is. I was the one who pushed for you to keep the kitten. I just thought after so much time went by that no one was going to claim him. And you two look so cute together. He clearly loves you."

She stopped and faced him. "Stop. You're just making this worse."

"I'm sorry." He wasn't good in emotional situations.

"And stop apologizing. I'll be fine. I'm better off alone. Besides, Cari will be back soon. I'll be so busy catching up with her that I won't even notice that Oreo isn't around." She turned, grabbed her stuff, and stormed off.

Did she really believe any of what she'd just said? Because he wasn't buying any of it. He knew how much she loved that kitten because even he had become fond of the little guy. He was going to miss him.

He couldn't stop blaming himself for the agony she was experiencing now. He'd encouraged her to bond with Oreo. He'd even insisted she give the kitten a name. At the time, he thought he was doing the right thing. He'd felt so bad for her being alone. He thought she and Oreo belonged together.

And now as he watched Sara head out the door to take the older couple to get Oreo, he wanted to do something to help her. He just didn't know how to fix this. He didn't even know if it was possible.

Chapter Sixteen

I T WAS FOR THE best.

Wednesday morning, Sara kept telling herself that after the Watsons came and took Oreo away. She liked her freedom. Now she didn't have to worry about anyone else. She could come and go as she pleased. No matter how many times she told herself that, she didn't believe any of it.

She hadn't realized how attached she'd become to Oreo until the little scamp was gone. Her apartment was filled with constant reminders of him from his colorful mice that he would bat around to the soft blanket she got for him to curl up in.

She'd been so upset last night that she hadn't answered the door when Kent stopped by. She was certain he was just there to give her words of comfort, and they would have only made her feel worse. It felt like everyone she loved eventually disappeared from her life.

And that was why when she listened to a voicemail from Kent, reminding her that he'd gone to the mainland for an in-person interview, she told herself it was for the best. She wasn't going to let herself care about him. She refused to acknowledge that it was already too late because somewhere between painting the walls and laying the flooring, he'd snuck past her carefully laid defenses. They had become more than friends, but she refused to name exactly what was between them.

She was actually relieved he wasn't at the inn that morning. It gave her time to pull herself together. And maybe this didn't have to be the end of her and Kent. After all Boston wasn't that far away. If he wanted, he could commute back and forth. Or even have an apartment in the city during the week and spend the weekend on the island.

Of course, she knew she was jumping ahead—way far ahead. He might not get the job, but then again she knew how bright he was. He would definitely get it. But he might not like the job and turn it down. Or he might realize that he was happiest here on the island—with her.

She halted her thoughts. She was letting herself daydream about something that wasn't going to happen. She knew not to count on people because they would leave her—sometimes through no fault of their own and other times by choice. The only person she could count on was herself.

And then she thought of Cari's impending return. She just wished she could get hold of her so she could get the details. She'd love to meet her at the airport. And there was the party she planned to throw. Today after work, she'd head into town and buy some decorations.

Their separation had been the longest ever. There was so much to catch up on. She knew her sister would ask about her and Kent. She had to figure out what to tell her.

And it had to be close to the truth because Cari was very good at reading her.

Sara picked up one of the photos to place on the wall. She carefully hooked it, making sure that it was level. Then she backed up to see what it looked like.

"Wow! This place is looking fantastic." The familiar voice came from behind her.

She paused and turned to find Harvey smiling proudly. He checked in most every day to see the progress. Next to him stood Kent's parents. She hadn't been expecting them. They stood quietly as they took in the transformation. Sara hoped they liked it.

"Oh, hi." She felt a bit awkward.

Kent's mother smiled at her. "You've done a fantastic job. I just know that Josie is going to love it."

"I hope so, but I can't take much of the credit. Kent did most of the work, and then we worked together to give the room a polished look. We're just working on the final details now. Well, Kent will help me when he gets back from his interview."

Both of Kent's parents looked surprised. *Oh no!* She'd said too much. Why hadn't Kent told her that it was a secret?

Mr. Turner cleared his throat. "Kent is interviewing for a job?"

Sara froze. Her heart pounded. What was she supposed to say now? It was far too late to walk back her words. Instead of opening her mouth, because she didn't trust her tongue at the moment, she wordlessly nodded.

"This job," Mrs. Turner said. "Is it for another refresh project?"

Sara carefully considered her next response. She opted once more for a wordless shake of her head.

"It's an accounting position, isn't it?" Mr. Turner's gaze searched hers.

Sara nodded. "I'm sorry. I didn't realize he hadn't told you." She wanted to ask them not to say anything to Kent about her spilling the news, but she knew from their shocked and now-worried looks that they'd never be able to keep from mentioning this to him. "He...he'll be back tomorrow night."

This time neither parent spoke. Sara turned a pleading gaze to Harvey. He was always good with people, and she could really use his help right now.

Harvey cleared his throat and stepped forward. "I can't get over the transformation of this room. It's so much brighter and welcoming." He glanced over at Kent's parents. "Don't you think so?"

It took a moment, but then Kent's mother said, "Oh, yes. It's wonderful. Josie is going to love this." She gently elbowed her husband. "Don't you like it?"

Mr. Turner nodded. "It feels a lot more open and welcoming."

Sara smiled and hoped to help smooth things over—at least a little bit. "Kent had the idea for the lighter shade of paint and flooring. I think it made a huge difference. And then I suggested doing away with the heavy drapes and instead using a white valance to let in as much sunlight as possible."

"I agree with you," Mrs. Turner said. "This room is huge, and it needs as much natural light as possible."

"Why don't you show them how you're arranging the photos?" Harvey gave her a nod.

"Sure. They are over here behind the display cases." She started toward the back of the room, all the while hoping the Turners would follow her. When she came to a stop and turned, she was relieved to find them right behind her.

She explained how she came up with the idea of framing the photos with some trim. She told them about painting the wood and adding the gold paint. They seemed impressed as they continued to ask her questions. The more Sara talked, the more at ease she became.

"The news has been making it around town." Sara wanted his parents to realize that their son had come up with an impressive idea. "In fact, we were over at the Seaside Bookshop, and Melinda is interested in having a nook installed in the front of the store." She failed to mention that some of the pieces Melinda wanted would have to be specially made.

"He tried to tell us about his concept," Mrs. Turner said, "but we had no idea that it would involve all of this. This is practically like a job all of its own."

"I don't understand," Mr. Turner said. "If he likes all of this." He waved his hand around at all of the renovations. "Why is he on the mainland interviewing for another job?"

Three pairs of eyes turned to Sara. She wanted to shrink down into the floorboards. "I...I don't know."

It was the truth. Sort of. She knew Kent was doing a lot of soul-searching—hunting for what would make him truly happy. Her guess was that he was very happy working in the family business, except for the part of his parents calling all of the shots, but there was no way she was going to point that out to them. That was a conversation Kent already had with them, and they didn't appear to be ready to change things.

His parents continued to look around. They seemed genuinely impressed with everything they'd done. When they'd made it the whole way around the room, they thanked her for showing them the room, and then they left.

Sara turned a worried look to Harvey. "That didn't go well."

"It could have been worse."

"I don't know how. And now when Kent gets back and finds out that I told his parents he was interviewing for another position, he'll be mad at me." The thought weighed on her.

"I wouldn't worry about it. If it was that big of a deal, he would have mentioned it was a secret. From my experience, nothing good ever comes from secrets." Harvey pressed a hand to his chest as his brows drew together and his lips pursed.

She stepped closer. "Are you okay?"

He nodded as he reached into his pocket and pulled out a roll of antacids. He popped a couple into his mouth. "I don't think the pizza I had for lunch agreed with me."

"Are you sure that's all it is?"

He nodded before sending her a reassuring smile. "I'm totally fine. Although I have to get back to work."

As Harvey strolled away, Sara was left wondering about his comments about nothing good ever coming from keeping secrets. Was he referring to Kent not telling his parents about his interview? Or was Harvey referring to something else—something like her growing feelings for Kent? No, it wasn't possible. She hadn't mentioned anything to him about the growing attraction between her and Kent. And that was the way it was going to remain.

———

It was complete.

It was a beautiful sunny Thursday afternoon with a gentle summer breeze. And the refreshed lobby was now open for business. Talk about a lot of foot traffic. The wedding party had already started to arrive.

Sara had just finished checking in the parents of the groom when a familiar face showed up. Sara made her way around the check-in desk and rushed toward Josie. "You're back."

"You make it sound like you had some doubt as to whether or not I'd return."

"Well...I mean, you do have a hunky guy on the West Coast who's crazy about you. It wouldn't be out of the realm of possibilities for you to decide that you can't live without him in your life and stay there."

Josie smiled. "Don't think the thought hadn't crossed my mind a few times—especially when he dropped me off at the airport."

"But you'll see him again soon, right?"

Josie nodded. "He'll be here in a couple of weeks. But enough about us. I can't believe this is the same lobby." She stepped farther into the room and let her gaze meander through the area. "When Kent first mentioned this refresh idea, I have to admit that I wasn't so sure about it. But this... Wow! You two really outdid yourselves."

Heat warmed Sara's cheeks. "I'm so glad you like it."

Josie glanced around. "Where's my brother? I thought he'd be here for the praise."

"I... I don't know where he is. I haven't seen him today." And she wasn't about to mention that he had an interview. She'd made that mistake once. She wasn't about to repeat it.

Josie stopped walking and turned to her. "You've gone above and beyond. I'm really impressed with all you've done. There'll be something extra in your next paycheck. And, I've been planning to do this, and now seems like the right time. I'm promoting you to manager."

Sara gasped. "You are?"

Josie smiled and nodded. "I've been watching the way you go out of your way for the guests. That's what makes this inn special. People remember when people are nice to them. It makes them want to keep coming back."

Her heart pitter-pattered. "Thank you so much. I won't let you down."

"I know you won't. And now that Lane is in my life, I'm going to need some flexibility in my schedule."

"No more working all day and all evening?"

"Not all of the time. Lane has been pressing me to find some balance in my life."

They continued to talk for a few more minutes. Sara caught her up on everything going on around the inn, and then she updated her on the Carrington wedding.

"Thank you, Sara. You've made my time away stress-free. And now you should start your vacation."

"But I'm not due to start it until next week."

"And I'm the boss, so I say go. Enjoy yourself. Consider this bonus time off."

"But the wedding..."

"Don't worry about it. You have everything under control. I'll take over now. I hope you have a wonderful vacation."

Sara wanted to tell her that she was canceling her vacation. With Oreo gone and Kent avoiding her, she didn't know what to do with herself. But she didn't want to explain any of this to Josie, who would undoubtedly have questions—lots of questions.

Instead Sara said, "Thank you so much. If there's anything you need? Or, if you have any questions, just call. I'll be around all week."

"I'll be fine. Enjoy the time off." And with that, Josie walked away.

Sara was left wondering what in the world she was going to do with all of her free time—time she would use to think about how much she missed Oreo and how much she was going to miss Kent when he moved to the mainland. And then there was the fact that her sister wasn't returning her calls. What was up with that?

Chapter Seventeen

H E'D NAILED THEM.

Friday morning, Kent was relieved to be back on the island. In the past couple of days, he'd had not one but two lengthy in-person interviews with multiple people at each company. The first had been in Boston, and the second one had been in Hartford. It was the Hartford position that offered him everything he could ask for, from his responsibilities to his benefits package. If he were to get the job, he'd be crazy not to take it.

Which brought him back to his biggest problem—leaving Bluestar. More pointedly, he didn't know if he was ready to leave Sara now that things between them were coming together. He wanted to see where their relationship was headed.

He'd gotten home a lot later last night than he'd hoped. Traffic had been snarled from a big accident. With the lateness of the hour, he hadn't made it to the inn to make sure the grand re-opening went smoothly. He owed Sara a big apology.

Showered and dressed, he headed out the door to go to Sara's place. He was hoping to catch her before work.

But as he headed out the walk, he ran into his father. His frowning father.

"Hey, Dad. What are you doing here?" He glanced at his watch. It was seven thirty-five. "Shouldn't you be at the store?"

"Your mother is opening up today. We need to talk."

He didn't like the sound of that. "Now's not a good time. I need to be somewhere."

"It looks like you're going to be late." His father had a no-nonsense attitude. The same one he had when Kent and his brothers broke the neighbor's back window with their baseball.

Kent smothered a groan as he retraced his steps to his apartment and unlocked the door. The only problem was that he had absolutely no idea what had put the frown lines on his father's face.

Once they were inside and the door closed, his father said, "When were you going to tell us?"

"Tell you what?"

"That you're moving and taking another job."

Whoa! How did they know? It took him a second, and then he realized the only person who knew about his interviews was Sara… But she wouldn't say anything. Would she?

There was absolutely no reason for him to deny it. Perhaps it was best to just get it out there. He knew his parents weren't going to like it. He wasn't sure he liked it, but he had to keep moving forward instead of being stuck in this rut.

He swallowed hard. "I was going to tell you when there was something to say."

The frown lines on his father's weathered face deepened. "So you weren't going to say anything until you had a new job."

Kent shifted his weight from one foot to the other. "Honestly, I don't know. I know I just can't keep doing the same thing over and over, day after day. I need new challenges."

His father didn't say anything for a moment. "And you can't do that at the store?"

"I tried. But you and Mom don't want any changes. My leaving is for the best. We can't keep butting heads at every turn. It isn't good for us, and it certainly isn't good for the business. I need to find a new path."

"Don't walk away." His father's eyes implored him. "We need you. This is a family business, and someday it'll be yours to run. Your brothers and sister don't have any interest in it."

His father knew exactly how to heap the guilt on him. It was something he'd been wrestling with for some time now. And he just couldn't cave in now—not if he wanted to be happy. "I'm sorry, Dad. I just can't go back to the way things were. I have to go."

He turned and headed out the door, leaving his father to come to terms with the changes that were about to happen in both of their lives. It was going to take some adjusting for the both of them.

He walked to Sara's place. He was filled with pent-up energy and frustration. The walk would do him good.

Although he was now later than he'd hoped, so he wasn't sure if he would be able to catch her before she left for work.

His strides were long and quick. He didn't stop to make conversation along his way, but the occasional good morning and hello were unavoidable. Though, he was in no mood to make small talk.

He had just reached the sidewalk in front of Sara's place when he spotted her. She'd just descended the steps from her second-story apartment. He waited for her at the end of the walkway.

When she spotted him, she smiled. He chose to ignore the way it caused his heart to skip a beat. Instead, he focused on how things were starting to spin out of control.

When she reached him, he asked, "How could you have done it?"

Confusion filled her eyes. "Done what?"

"Told my parents I was on a job interview?"

"That's what you're mad at me about?"

He pressed his hands to his sides. "Yes."

Her brows drew together. "You never told me it was a secret, and I didn't do it intentionally. It wasn't until the words were out that I realized your parents didn't know about your plans. But is it really such a big deal? They had to be told eventually. Right?"

He raked his fingers through his hair. He didn't know what to say to that. It would be better if he wasn't so torn about his decision to stay or go.

"Kent, what's going on?" Her gaze searched his. "Did you change your mind about moving away?"

Was that hope he saw twinkle in her eye? In a blink, it was gone. She stood there, looking expectantly.

Buzz.

It was his phone. For once, he was relieved by the interruption. "Sorry. I have to get this."

When he retrieved his phone, he saw that it was the employer in Hartford. He expected Sara to head off to work, but she continued to stand there. It appeared she really wanted an answer from him.

He pressed the phone to his ear. The conversation was short and to the point. They'd narrowed their list of candidates to him and one other person. They wanted him to come back in for another interview as soon as possible. He told them he was available that afternoon, and they said they'd make it work.

Once he disconnected the call, Sara said, "Was it good news?"

"It could be. I made the shortlist of candidates. I have to go back for another interview."

Was that a flicker of disappointment in her eyes? In a heartbeat, it was replaced with a smile that didn't quite reach her eyes. "Congratulations."

"I didn't get the job."

"Yet... But you will. How could they not hire you? You're good at everything you do."

"Not everything." Finding it hard to stay mad at her, he decided to lighten the mood. "You don't want to see me try to bake anything. It ends up in a big flour cloud and a mess all over the kitchen."

Her brows rose. "Surely it's not that bad."

"If you don't believe me, I can come inside and demonstrate."

"Um...no. I'll pass on that." And then not sure what to talk about, he said, "I won't keep you."

As he walked away, he heard her call out, "Good luck."

He paused and turned. "Thank you."

She turned and headed in the opposite direction. As much as he wanted to stay angry with her for telling his parents, she was right. They had to be told sooner rather than later.

The problem was that leaving the island was getting harder and harder. As he stood there watching Sara's fading form, he realized she was the main reason he didn't want to go.

A vacation day.

And Sara had no idea what to do with herself. She wasn't used to having nothing to do. Usually when she wasn't working at the inn, she was reading out on her deck. But she couldn't sit still long enough to read. Her mind wouldn't settle. It kept going over her last conversation with Kent.

He'd been angry with her for letting his job search slip to his parents, but by the time he departed, it felt as though he wasn't so angry with her any longer. At least that was what she hoped.

She headed for the beach. She normally found the sound of the sea and the call of the birds relaxing. She loved to feel the sand between her toes and then the rush of the surf over them.

She tried to come up with something to do on this unexpected free day. And then it came to her. She could work on cleaning her sister's apartment and getting it ready for Cari's arrival.

Just as quickly, she recalled that her sister hadn't emailed the signed agreement. What was up with that?

Sara reached for her phone and hit redial. She knew her sister was busy with the big move, but she had to stop long enough to do the paperwork. Sara worried that Kent wouldn't hang onto the apartment much longer. And with a housing shortage on the island, the place would go in a heartbeat.

The phone rang once and then twice with no answer. She wasn't going to hang up until it went to voicemail. And so it continued to ring.

"Hello." The female voice sounded distant like she was talking down a long tunnel.

"Cari?" Sara wanted to make sure it was actually her sister because the connection wasn't so good.

"Of course. You're the one who called me. Remember?"

That was definitely her sister. Sara smiled. "Sorry. This isn't a good connection. I just called to see if you'd returned the lease for the apartment yet."

There was a long pause. She started to wonder if they'd lost their connection. It wouldn't be the first time for their calls to be disconnected.

"Cari, are you still there?"

"Yes. I've been meaning to call you. I have some news."

News? What sort of news? She couldn't make out her sister's voice well enough to figure out if it was good news or bad news. Her chest tightened. *Please don't let it be bad news.*

"What sort of news?" The breath caught in her lungs.

"I've met someone."

That didn't sound like bad news. "I'm happy for you. Can't wait to meet him."

"About that...um, I'm not moving back to the island."

The unexpected words hit Sara like an emotional sucker punch. It knocked the air from her lungs as her stomach gave a nauseous lurch. This couldn't be right. Her sister wouldn't let her down.

Another long silence ensued as Sara replayed her sister's words. This time the silence was strained as a million thoughts raced through Sara's mind. This wasn't possible. This was her sister's bad attempt at some sort of joke.

"Of course you're coming home. We haven't seen each other in a few years, and the apartment is available."

"Sara, I'm not coming. Things with Adam are serious."

"Serious?" Her voice rose. People on the beach glanced in her direction. She forced her voice to a lower volume. "How long have you known..." She struggled to remember the guy's name.

"Adam," Cari supplied. "We met a few weeks ago."

A few weeks? Sara's mind raced. "So, you knew him when you asked me to get you the apartment?"

"Yes. But it's not like you think. He had a girlfriend at the time. And I had no reason to think anything would happen between us."

"Cari, how could you do this to me?" Tears of anger and frustration stung the back of her eyes. "You have no idea what I did to get you that apartment."

"I'm sorry. I didn't know this was going to happen."

There had to be a way to salvage this. "Bring him home with you."

"No. He has a job here, and he can't leave." Her answer was succinct, leaving no room for rebuttal.

"So that's it?"

"I'm sorry, Sara. Really, I am. Can you do something for me? Can you let Kent know that I'm passing on the apartment?"

Really? After everything, she still wanted Sara to do her a favor. Well, she was done jumping through hoops to make people happy. "No, Cari, I won't do that. This is your problem. You need to fix it. I've got to go."

Sara ended the call. Her breathing came in rapid gasps. Her mind spun with all that had just happened. Her heart ached as tears splashed onto her cheeks. She dashed them away.

She couldn't believe this was happening to her again. She had been counting on her sister to do what she'd said and move home. Why had she let herself get caught up in something she should have known wouldn't happen?

It was like as soon as she cared about someone, they drifted out of her life. First, her mother, then her father, then Cari, now Oreo and Kent. Because she was certain he was going to get the job on the mainland, and there would be no reason for him to stay.

Having absolutely no destination in mind and nowhere she wanted to be, she found herself walking back to her place. She ended up with an iced tea and a mystery book on her deck. She forced herself to concentrate on the words on the page instead of the mess otherwise known as her life.

Slowly, word by word, sentence by sentence, she let the sun's rays soothe her. When her thoughts strayed to Kent, she would lose her place in the story, but she'd circle back and reread that part.

The more she read, the better she felt. Reading had been her escape after her mother died. She'd read everything she could get her hands on. And then again after her father passed. With every traumatic event in her life, she would slip away into a story until she was calm enough to deal with the fallout in her own life.

Hours later, she set aside the now-finished book. The sun was sinking low in the sky. Though her heart felt battered and bruised, she was able to focus on her own life. She'd just received a promotion at the inn. She needed to focus on the good things in her life and not the holes in her heart. Going forward she needed to protect herself and not let people get close to her.

CHAPTER EIGHTEEN

H E SHOULD BE ON top of the world.

That evening Kent returned to Bluestar Island. This week had been full of twists and turns. His head was still spinning with all of the events.

He had big news. And the first person he wanted to share it with was Sara. He'd never felt the need to share something like this with someone else before.

No matter how much he wanted to deny it, Sara was special. Sure the beginning of their story had been rocky, but somewhere along the way, things had changed between them. Instead of the hostility that had ebbed between them, it had been replaced with a flow of friendship—and perhaps more. His steps came quicker. Was it possible Sara felt the same way toward him?

When he reached the steps to Sara's apartment, he took them two at a time. They'd been floating and dancing around the subject of them for long enough. It was time to be honest with each other.

He stepped onto the landing and moved to the door. His knuckles rapped on the door. *Please be home.*

As though in answer to his wish, the door opened. Sara stood there with a neutral look on her face. "Kent, now isn't a good time."

"But I have news."

"That's nice, but I'm not the one you should be talking to. I'm sure your parents would like to hear the news."

"They can wait. Please let me in."

She didn't move, and he was starting to think she wasn't going to move. But he wasn't going to just walk away. It was important they speak.

With a sigh, Sara opened the door for him to enter. It was progress. He moved into the middle of the room. He noticed that she left the door open as she turned to face him. Was that her way of letting him know that as soon as he had his say he was being kicked to the curb?

He ignored the implication and instead focused on the reason for his visit. "I got the job."

The neutral expression remained on her face. "Congratulations."

He noticed how her one-word response lacked any emotion. "Thank you. I'm supposed to start in a couple of weeks."

For a moment, she didn't respond. She stepped back to the open doorway and leaned against it. "When do you leave?"

"I don't know. I haven't accepted the position yet."

"You should. It's the new beginning you were looking for."

He stepped closer to her. "It is but what about us?"

She shook her head. "There is no us."

"But what about the time we spent together? And the kiss we shared?"

She glanced away. "It was nothing serious. It was us just getting caught up in the moment. Don't let that hold you back. Our job at the inn is over. Your sister is back and loves the refresh."

He was surprised by her rejection. This was not what he'd been expecting. "You can't be serious."

"About what?"

He stepped up to her and stared into her eyes. "About us."

Her gaze was unwavering. "I'm very serious. You aren't the only one who has their career to think about. I've just been promoted to manager of the inn, so with the increased responsibilities I won't have much free time for a social life."

He stepped back as though her words had smacked him in his face. "I must have read things wrong."

She shrugged. "I'm sure you'll meet someone new in Boston."

"Actually it's Hartford."

There was a flicker of something in her eyes, but it was gone before he was able to decipher it. "You should go now."

There was a part of him that felt as though he should say something more, but what was left to say? He'd totally read the situation wrong. Very wrong.

Buzz.

It wasn't his phone. His gaze moved to Sara. She pulled the phone from her back pocket. When she glanced at the caller ID, she frowned.

"Something wrong?" He knew it was none of his business, but he couldn't stop caring about Sara so quickly.

"It's the people who took Oreo."

The phone continued to ring.

"You should answer it."

She pressed the phone to her ear. There were a lot of one-word answers. The color drained from her face. It left him even more curious.

When she ended the call, he looked at her expectantly. She didn't say anything, forcing him to speak up. "Is everything okay with the kitten?"

"No. Oreo ran away again. They called here to see if I'd seen him."

Concern had him stepping back toward the doorway. "How long has he been gone?"

"They aren't sure, but the last time they saw him was this morning when they fed him."

"Poor little guy. I bet he's getting hungry."

"And he's probably scared."

For the moment, their concern about Oreo trumped their prior conversation. They needed to find the kitten and quickly as nighttime wasn't far off.

Without a word, Sara ran back to her bedroom.

"Sara, where are you going? We need to start searching."

She rushed back to the living room with her shoes in her hand. She dropped them on the floor and slipped her feet into them. "I needed some shoes. And what is this about *we* need to start searching?"

"I'm going to help."

"But it's not your problem. You have other things to do."

"The only thing I have to do right now is to find Oreo."

Sara wasn't the only one who had become fond of the kitten. Oreo was full of personality. Kent never thought of himself as a cat person before, but that little furball had definitely changed his mind.

And there was the worried look written all over Sara's face. Maybe he'd read things wrong between them, but it didn't mean he wouldn't help her out when she needed him. And right now she needed a lot of help because even though this was a small island for humans, when it came to little kittens, it could be huge.

Poor Oreo.

Sara's heart went out to the curious kitten, who had gotten himself lost. She should tell Kent to move on, but she needed all of the help possible to find the little kitten. Nothing could happen to him. Nothing at all.

She turned to Kent. "What are you doing just standing there?"

"Okay then." He moved swiftly down the stairs.

She was right behind him. At the bottom of the stairs, she spotted Birdie out on her porch. She rushed over. "Have you seen Oreo?"

"Oreo? I thought he went back to his owners."

"He did, but he ran away earlier today, and they called me to see if I'd seen him."

Birdie got to her feet. Ever since she'd broken her hip, she moved a little slower, but she didn't let it stop her. "No. I haven't seen him." She glanced up at the sky. "The sun will be setting in a couple of hours. You don't have much time to search for him. I'll make some phone calls."

"Thank you. I doubt he can find his way back here, but I'd appreciate if you could keep an eye out."

"I will. I hope you find him."

"Me too."

Sara made her way back to the roadway. She didn't see Kent and couldn't help but feel disappointed that he'd left. Although there was no reason for him to stay, especially not after their conversation.

He was definitely leaving. The pain was too much. If she delved into her feelings now, she'd fall apart. She couldn't let that happen. Oreo needed her to keep it together. She shoved the emotions to the back of her mind.

She focused on little Oreo. She had to find him. She started back on the pathway between her place and Birdie's that led to the beach. It was there that she ran into Kent.

"Oh. I thought you left."

He frowned at her. "You aren't the only one who cares about Oreo. I want to see him safe just as much as you do."

They set off together, working their way down to the beach. They moved slowly as they checked behind each rock and bush. The only talking they did was about the kitten.

Once they'd explored the beach area, they headed toward town—toward Oreo's other home. Maybe he was somewhere in between them. After all, he was just a little kitten. How far could he get?

But then she thought of how energetic the kitten was when he'd lived with her. He was a little ball of energy. Maybe she was underestimating him.

As they made their way into town, they passed a lot of people who were out and about. They were searching under shrubs and in every nook and corner. Sara was touched by all of the people who were helping with the search—even Agnes Dewey was searching for the kitten.

All the while the sun was sinking farther in the sky. "We aren't going to find him tonight."

"Hey, don't give up." Kent reached out and squeezed her hand.

The touch sent a shiver up her arm that set her heart pitter-pattering. It would be so easy to turn to him and find comfort in his arms, but she couldn't give in to that desire. It would only complicate this already messy relationship.

She grudgingly withdrew her hand. As soon as her hand was free of his, the place he'd been touching suddenly felt cold. She regretted pulling away, even if it was for the best.

CHAPTER NINETEEN

THEY WERE RUNNING OUT of time.

Kent hadn't said it to Sara, but if they didn't find the kitten soon, they were going to have to stop until the morning. He knew how worried Sara was. When she called out for Oreo, there was a desperation in her voice that went far beyond the normal reaction to a missing pet.

He had no idea how much she loved and missed Oreo. Sure, he was fond of the kitten, but it didn't go nearly as deep as Sara's feelings. It was a shame the Watsons had wanted the kitten back. Maybe once the kitten was found, they'd reconsider and let the kitten live with Sara.

They'd searched all over Bluestar; at least that was the way it felt. They'd worked their way to Beachcomber Park. They weren't the only people searching the area. It was a large park, so the more help, the better.

So many people were out searching. It felt as though the whole town had come out to help. It was amazing what Bluestar could accomplish when they all pulled together. He couldn't help but think how much he would miss this town with its giant heart. But now that Sara had pushed him away and basically told him that what they had was nothing more than a good time, he didn't have anything holding him back. Tomorrow, he'd call the Hartford company back and let them know he'd be taking the job.

The thought of moving to Hartford was taking a lot to get used to the idea. He told himself it would be good for him. Then his gaze would stray to Sara, and his heart would feel at odds with his mind. Why was she working so hard to push him away?

He shoved aside the troubling thoughts as he paused to search some shrubbery. When he straightened, he noticed Sara a little ways off. Even the mayor was out and about. Mayor Banks paused to offer Sara some words of encouragement. Kent knew everyone was there to help Sara. People loved her, and it was so easy to do. Sara was kind and thoughtful, which made him wonder why she was suddenly being so cold to him.

He moved toward her. He thought of asking if she'd found anything, but he knew that was pointless. He knew if she had a lead on the kitten that she would have let him know. The problem was that he was running out of encouraging words as the shadows grew long.

When he glanced over at her for the hundredth time, he saw her swipe at her cheek. His heart broke for her. Oreo just had to turn up.

"Why don't we split up?" he suggested. "You head back to your place and look around. I'll continue to search the park." When she stood there quietly, as though debating if she should leave or not, he said, "Go ahead. We've got it." He gestured to all of the other people calling for Oreo and searching high and low. "It's going to be okay."

"Do you really believe that?" Her voice wavered with emotion.

"Yes, I do." He stepped toward her to give her a hug, but she stepped back. He restrained a frustrated sigh. He hated that she'd put up a wall between them that he couldn't scale. "Go on. I'll catch up with you shortly."

She nodded and then turned around. As she made her way along the sidewalk, her head moved from side to side as she continued the search for Oreo.

He checked his phone's battery. It was starting to get down there, since he'd been using the flashlight app in order to look in the shadows. If he were a kitten, where would he go?

The only answer he came up with was back to Sara. Oreo had seemed so happy living with her. It would seem natural that if the kitten was lost he'd try to get back to Sara where he felt safe and happy.

But they'd thoroughly checked around her building and the path where they'd originally found Oreo. There had been no sign of him. And so Kent continued his search of the far end of the park.

Buzz.

The phone was already in his hand as he needed the flashlight app constantly now that the sun had sunk beneath the horizon. He hoped the call was from Sara and that she had good news. Instead, he found the caller was Sara's sister. Perhaps Cari was calling to let him know she had emailed the lease. And he would inform her that he was handing all of that business over to his parents now that he'd gotten a new job.

He pressed the phone to his ear. "Hello."

"Hey, Kent. It's Cari. First, I want to thank you for holding the apartment for me. I appreciate it so much."

"No problem. But it isn't me you should thank. It's your sister. Sara made it all possible."

"You mean by asking you?"

"Well, that too." He was confused. "Didn't she tell you about our deal?"

"No."

He was surprised that Sara hadn't mentioned their endeavor. And so he proceeded to tell her about their deal for her to help him with the inn's refresh in exchange for him leasing the apartment to her sister.

"I can't believe she did all of that for me. I... I feel awful for changing my plans."

Her last words caught him off guard. "Changed your plans?"

"Oh. Yes. The reason I'm calling you is to tell you how much I appreciate everything you've done for me. And to let you know that I'm not returning to the island."

This was the last thing he expected to hear. "Does Sara know?"

"Yes. We spoke a little bit ago. I explained it all to her." There was a voice in the background, but he couldn't make out what they were saying. "I have to go now. Thanks again."

And then the line went dead. Kent stood there for a moment absorbing what he'd just learned. Then Sara's frostiness started to make sense.

She must feel like she keeps losing the people she cares about. First, the kitten going back to live with the Watsons. Then her sister blows her off. And now he tells her that he might move to the mainland. When he put it that way, it made sense that she would put up her guard with him.

This was a nightmare.

Sara would do anything to find Oreo and return him to his home. But it was worrisome that he was able to escape twice now. This time she hoped the Watsons would take some precautions to keep him from getting out.

She appreciated her neighbors and friends helping out with the search, especially Kent. He certainly didn't have to help. In fact, she wouldn't have blamed him if he had kept walking when she'd first received the call about Oreo having gone missing.

And yet he'd stayed. She so desperately wanted to lean on him, but she wouldn't give herself the luxury. It would just be delaying the inevitable—him leaving the island. She just couldn't set herself up to get hurt worse.

She searched as best she could in the fading sunlight as she made her way home. In front of her apartment she came across Birdie taking Peaches for a walk.

"Any luck?" Birdie asked.

Sara shook her head as she came to a stop. She crouched down to pet Peaches. "Thank you for calling people and getting them to help with the search. With so many people looking, you would have thought we would have located him by now." She straightened. "I just can't imagine where he's hiding."

"He'll turn up when he's ready. Probably when his hunger is stronger than his fear of humans."

"I bet you're right." She'd get a can of cat food out of the donation bag that she had stuffed in her closet and open it. Maybe if she put it near the bottom of her steps, he'd come out of hiding. At this point, she was willing to try most anything to find him.

"When will your sister arrive?" Birdie asked.

"Oh. Um... She's not coming back to Bluestar." When Birdie's eyes widened with surprise, Sara said, "She met someone in Malaysia."

"Ahh... I see. I'm sorry she won't be back, but I'm happy to hear that she's found love. It's a powerful thing. In fact, it was love that brought me to Bluestar Island for the first time."

"You mean you weren't born here?" When Birdie shook her head, Sara said, "I didn't know that. I thought you'd always lived here."

"I was born and raised in New York. I only moved to the island after meeting my husband at the World's Fair. So, it was love that brought me to the island. Sometimes you have to follow your heart. Love isn't always easy but if it's right, it's worth the sacrifices."

Sara couldn't help but wonder if Birdie was talking about her own relationship or Sara's relationship with Kent. She'd never considered moving away from Bluestar. It had always been her home. She immediately dismissed the idea. She couldn't imagine ever calling someplace else her home.

There was a squeak or was it a cry. It was soft as though it was off in the distance. It was so faint that for a moment Sara wondered if she'd imagined it.

She looked at Birdie. "Did you hear that?"

"Hear what, dear?"

Sara was quiet for a moment. The breath stilled in her lungs as she strained to hear the sound once more. There was nothing. She released her pent-up breath.

"I thought it was Oreo, but I don't hear it now."

"My hearing isn't as good as it used to be, but if you heard him, I believe you. Maybe he's on the path to the beach. You should go check."

"I think I will." With a wave she was off.

She reached the sidewalk leading to her apartment. "Oreo?" She called out softly, not wanting to scare him. "Oreo, are you out here?"

It was so hard to see now that the sun had set. And her phone was dead. She rushed up the steps to her place. Once she dropped her phone on the charger, she headed for the closet. She yanked out the bag of kitten stuff that she had been procrastinating about donating. She grabbed a can of moist kitten food. And in her kitchen drawer, she retrieved a flashlight.

She dashed back out the door and down the steps. She stopped at the bottom. "Oreo, dinner." She popped the lid on the can. The sound was one he'd learned to love. He knew when he heard it that soon he'd have something delicious to eat. "Oreo, come eat."

She placed the can on the sidewalk and sat down on a step. She thought of turning on the flashlight, but if he was around, she didn't want to scare him off. She knew he must have had a very traumatic day.

One minute turned into two minutes. She was beginning to think this idea wasn't going to work either. And yet she continued to sit there and mentally will the little guy to come to her.

When she lifted her head to the sky, she spotted a star. It was the first star of the night, and so, she did something she hadn't done since she was a kid—she wished upon a star.

The next thing she knew, she heard a strange sound. It wasn't a cry or meow. It sounded more like someone or something was eating. She lowered her head and squinted into the shadows.

There was definitely something there. Was it Oreo? She pressed the end of the flashlight to her leg and turned it on. She wanted to be cautious with the light so she didn't scare them off.

As she raised the light, she averted it from the sidewalk. In the glow of the beam, she was at last able to make out the kitten licking at the can of food. It was Oreo.

She stifled an excited squeal. Her heart leapt with joy. He was safe. *Thank goodness*. She wanted to run over to him and scoop him up in her arms, but she was worried that in the dark, any quick movements might scare him.

And so she started by talking softly to him. "Hey, Oreo, it's me."

He kept right on eating. She slowly stood. One cautious step after the next, she made her way to him. "You're a hungry little fella, aren't you? You probably didn't have anything to eat all day. You shouldn't have run away. Anything could have happened to you."

She knelt down next to him and ran her hand over his back. His downy fur was coated with sand and other debris. As she pet him, his deep purr vibrated through his body. She smiled as tears of joy clouded her vision.

When he stopped eating, she picked him up and snuggled him to her neck. "I've missed you."

His cold, damp nose touched her neck. It was as though he were saying he'd missed her too. With the kitten in one hand and the food in the other hand, she made her way up the steps to her apartment.

Once she fussed over Oreo, she got him some water. He eagerly lapped it up. With his thirst quenched, Oreo made his way to the couch and made himself comfortable right in the center of it, just as he had done when he'd lived with her. She wondered if he remembered his time with her.

As soon as he was settled, his eyes drifted closed. He looked utterly exhausted. The poor little guy. As she watched him breathe, tears blurred her vision. Her heart swelled with love. She was so relieved that Oreo was safe and sound. Now all she wanted to do was keep him.

There was just something so comforting about having the little guy around.

She retrieved her phone from the charger. It had just enough battery power to place a couple of calls. Her first call was to Birdie so she could tell everyone that Oreo had shown up. Birdie sounded just as excited as Sara felt. Birdie was never one for a quick chat, so they talked for a few more minutes. A warning beep from her phone let Sara know she was just about out of battery power. It was the perfect excuse to get off the phone.

It looked like it would be a little longer until she could call Kent and then the Watsons. Sara wasn't all that upset as she placed her phone back on the charger.

Knock-knock.

She moved to the door and opened it to find Kent standing there with a frown on his face. "I'm sorry, Sara. I've been looking everywhere, and I haven't found Oreo."

"It's okay. I was just about to call you, but my phone died."

"You found Oreo?"

She smiled and nodded. "It's more like he found me." She opened the door wider so he could step inside. "The poor little guy wore himself out making his way here."

Kent's gaze moved around the room until it came to rest on the couch. "I think I can hear him snoring from here."

"He ate and drank. Then he jumped, well, it was more like climbed up the couch and settled in for a long nap."

"It looks like he could stay right there the rest of the night."

"I wish. But I have to call the Watsons and let them know that he's been found."

Kent went over to the kitten and pet him. Oreo lifted his head. His eyelids were heavy, as though it were an ordeal to lift them. "Are you sure he's okay?"

"As sure as I can be. Other than being a bit dirty, he appears tired, but that's all."

Kent straightened and moved away from the couch, letting Oreo go back to sleep. "I'm glad you found him."

"Actually, he found me. And I'm so relieved." Her gaze met his. "Thank you for dropping everything to help me search for him. I really appreciate it."

"No problem. You know I'd do anything to help you."

His softly spoken words chipped away at the wall she'd erected around her heart. It would be so easy to give in to her desires and wrap her arms around him, but it would only be momentary. She refused to settle for scraps of his attention and time.

She leveled her shoulders and lifted her chin ever so slightly. "Well, it's been a long day. I'm sure you're tired after everything."

His brows momentarily rose. "Are you sure you don't want me to stick around and be here when the Watsons pick up Oreo?"

She shook her head. "I've got it."

His gaze searched hers. "Maybe we should talk. You know...about us."

Again she shook her head. "We've already said everything we need to say."

"What if I was to turn down the job and stay here?"

It was what she so desperately wanted to hear, but she knew the remedy to their situation wasn't that easy. "And what would you do then? Go back to your family's business and continue to do the same thing?"

A flicker of a frown came over his face. "I can make it work."

She knew he was lying to himself and her. And though it touched her that he was willing to even consider this scenario, she knew it was untenable. Eventually, he would come to resent her for forcing him to give up an amazing job and be stuck in a position in his family's business that he'd outgrown. She couldn't let that happen. She didn't want to make him miserable.

"Go start your new job." She struggled to keep the emotion from her voice. "You'll do great."

"But..."

"Please just go." She didn't know how long she could hold out if he were to keep talking.

He exhaled a resigned sigh. He turned and walked away. When she closed the door, she leaned back against it and closed her eyes. That had been one of the hardest things she'd ever had to do, but it was the right thing to do for Kent.

Gathering herself, she straightened. She headed for the kitchen counter. She grabbed her partially charged phone and moved to the couch. She sat down next to Oreo. When she ran her hand over his back, he woke up. He immediately crawled onto her lap and went to sleep.

She wished she could sit there the rest of the evening and hold him. And yet she knew what she had to do next. She lifted her phone and began to dial.

CHAPTER TWENTY

H E WASN'T READY TO go home.

Kent kept walking. He was upset with the way Sara had so readily dismissed him. They had things to discuss. In truth, he wasn't sure who he was more upset with—her for acting like what they'd shared was so easily dismissed or himself for falling for her. It was the exact thing he told himself he wasn't going to do.

Right now, he should be on top of the world. He'd just landed a high-paying job with benefits. It would place him on the career ladder where he could keep climbing and challenging himself. And now Sara had stumbled into his life and had him rethinking everything.

If he went home now, he knew he'd do nothing more than pace around his apartment. He needed something to take his mind off his problems.

He reached for his phone and pulled up his brother Liam's number. The phone rang once and then twice. "Hey, bro, what's wrong?"

"Why does there have to be something wrong for me to call you?" Kent continued walking with no particular destination in mind.

"There doesn't. It's just that I figured you'd be busy with Sara. Seems like you two are spending all of your time together these days. Even Mom and Dad have noticed."

"I don't want to talk about it." And then he realized his brother might have his three-year-old son this weekend. "Do you have Tate?"

"No. He's with his mother. But I'll have him for the rest of the summer because she's off to Chile."

"Chile? What's she going to do there?"

"What she loves most in life—skiing."

"In July?"

"Yep. It's called Valle...something or other. It's her first visit there, and she's all excited about it. I'm looking forward to having Tate."

"Don't forget to schedule in some Uncle Kent time."

"I won't. So what's bothering you tonight?"

"Why do you think something is bothering me?"

"Because you have that grumpy tone in your voice."

"I do not." Did he?

"Oh, yes, you do. Trust me. I know all about that tone. I heard it all of the time when you would watch me, Jack, and Owen while Mom and Dad went to the store. So what gives?"

A smile pulled at the corners of Kent's mouth. Leave it to a sibling to know him so well and remind him of times he'd otherwise forgotten. "I'm just going to say that you three were always into something."

"Uh-huh. But we're not talking about me. We're discussing you. I heard you had an interview. Didn't it go well?"

Why wasn't he surprised his brother would know about his interview? It seemed as though there were no secrets in Bluestar. "For your information, it was technically three interviews for two different companies."

"Well, that sounds positive. Was it?"

Kent nodded but when he realized his brother couldn't see him, he said, "Yes. I just had a second interview this afternoon."

"And?"

"And I got the job." He went on to tell him some of the details of the position.

"That's awesome! Congrats!" After a moment of silence, Liam said, "Congratulations are in order, aren't they?"

Kent found himself heading toward the beach. He was relieved this conversation was taking place over the phone instead of in person so his brother couldn't read his facial expressions. Liam already read too much into his words.

"That's just it. I don't know." Kent sighed as he stared at the moon. "I thought I knew what I wanted, and then Sara happened into my life, and now I don't know what I want."

Liam let out a laugh.

Kent's body tensed. "This isn't funny."

"Yes, it is. My big brother is in love, and you don't even know it."

"I am not." The denial was quick and short.

"You do realize I don't believe you, right?"

Kent inwardly groaned. Why did he think talking to his brother was a good idea? He should have just gone home and kept this all to himself.

Liam subdued his amusement. "Kent, relax. So what's the problem? Doesn't she feel the same way?"

"I... I don't know. But it doesn't matter because if I take the job, I'll be in Connecticut, and she'll be here on the island."

"Then don't take the job."

"And then I'll be stuck in the office of the furniture store with absolutely no say in the business. It's the reason I started searching for a new job."

Liam was quiet for a moment. "So that's the problem. You're stuck choosing between the new job and the new lady in your life."

It was as though Liam had finally shined a light on the exact problem. "Yes. And I have absolutely no idea what to do about it."

"I wish I could give you some sort of advice, but I don't have any to give you. I've already made a mess of my own marriage."

Liam and his high school sweetheart had gotten married after a long engagement. They seemed so happy at first. And then things unraveled as they sometimes do. Now they were divorced with shared custody of their son.

Kent wrapped up the phone call, not sure if it had helped him with his problem or not. Because he knew if he went to Connecticut, he would always wonder what would have happened if he had stayed here on the island with Sara. And if he stayed here, he would be sentencing himself to more years of the exact same thing at work with no chance to expand the business because his parents were opposed to anything that represented a change.

So what was he to do? He didn't have the answer, but he had until Monday to give his potential employer an answer to their job offer.

ele

Her world had imploded.

The next morning Sara refused to stay at home and pull the blankets over her head. She forced herself to get a shower, style her hair, and put on some makeup. It made her feel a tiny bit better.

She didn't have an appetite, so she skipped breakfast. She grabbed a book and moved to the deck, hoping the sunshine would improve her mood.

The Watsons had picked up Oreo the prior evening, so he wasn't around to distract her, and she didn't have to go to the inn, because she was on vacation. Why did she think it was a good idea to plan some time off?

The sunshine warmed her, and eventually, she found herself getting lost in the words on the page. Before she knew it, she had finished the book she'd started the other day. It was time for a new book or two or three. Was it possible to have too many books? Sara didn't think so as she walked past her wall of built-in bookcases, which held all of her keepers—the books she could read over and over again.

She headed out the door on a mission. She'd spent many hours in the Seaside Bookshop. She loved the place, but tried not to go right after her payday or else she'd spend a small fortune. Today wasn't payday, so she was safe.

She took her time walking through Bluestar. She stopped repeatedly to thank people for helping with the search for Oreo and updating them on his discovery and his return to the Watsons.

It was quite a while until she reached the bookshop. In fact, it was lunchtime. Sara stepped up to the bookshop just as Melinda flipped the sign to read: *Back in 30 minutes*. Melinda stepped out the door and immediately spotted Sara. She held up a finger for Sara to wait just a moment.

Once the door was locked, Melinda joined her on the sidewalk. "Hi. I was just headed to lunch."

"Mind if I join you?"

"Not at all. I was just going to suggest it." After talking with so many people in town, Sara found her appetite was slowly coming back.

"I was just about to head over to the Lighthouse."

"Sounds good."

Melinda fell into step with her. "I heard you had quite a night with Oreo."

She nodded. "I was starting to think we'd never find him. He actually showed up at my place. I was so happy to see him. He was all dirty and hungry. He eventually fell asleep on the couch until the Watsons came to pick him up."

"I bet it was really hard to give him back."

"It was the hardest thing. All I wanted to do was keep him safe. How in the world does he keep escaping? It's like he's taken tips from Dash." When Melinda gave her a confused look, she said, "You know, Sam Bell's little pygmy goat."

"Oh yeah. The goat that visits town every few months."

"And yet Sam and Aster have done everything to keep Dash in his pen, but he always finds an escape."

"But did Oreo ever escape from your place?" Melinda arched a brow.

"No. He didn't."

"Maybe the only reason he keeps running away is because he's trying to find his home. Sounds like he had a good one with you."

"I liked to think so, but he belongs with the Watsons."

"Did you talk to them about it?"

Sara shook her head. "I wanted to, but it just didn't seem right."

They continued on to the Lighthouse Café, all the while making small talk. The restaurant was crowded, but they timed it just right and got the next available booth. They slid into their seats, and within a couple of minutes the server took their drink order.

"What are you going to eat?" Melinda stared down at the menu.

"I don't know." She browsed the menu but couldn't make up her mind. Eventually, she opted to get a chef salad, the same order as Melinda.

Every time the door to the restaurant opened, she would glance up, hoping it would be Kent. When it wasn't him, a sense of disappointment would come over her. It wasn't like they had anything left to say to each other, but that didn't keep her from wishing there was a way for them to be happy together.

"Instead of waiting and hoping you see him, why don't you call him?" Melinda's voice drew her from her thoughts.

Heat warmed Sara's cheeks. "What are you talking about?"

"You don't think I know that you're looking for Kent."

"Why do you think that?"

"Because I was talking to his brother Liam this morning, and he mentioned this new job of Kent's was coming between the two of you."

"No, it's not. I mean there's nothing between us."

"Uh-huh." Melinda nodded, but the look in her eyes said she didn't believe her.

Sara sighed. In between receiving their ice teas and then their chef salads, she told Melinda about what had gone on between her and Kent. She had hoped that talking about it would make her feel better, but it only made her feel worse.

"I don't know why any of this is bothering me. It's not like we were a couple or anything." Sara played with the wrapper from the straw.

Softly Melinda said, "It's because you love him."

"I do not." She said it with more emphasis than she'd intended. When Melinda once more arched a brow, Sara stopped and thought about it. She'd been denying her feelings for him for so long she didn't realize when she'd fallen for him.

Just then the server brought their checks. They each paid cash, and the server departed.

"You should tell him," Melinda said as though she could read Sara's thoughts.

"Even if I did love him, and I'm not saying that I do, he's moving to Connecticut to start a new job. It's too late."

"It's never too late."

"I don't want to come between him and this opportunity. He would eventually resent me for holding him back."

Melinda checked the time on her phone. "I need to be going. But I want to leave you with this last thought. Why can't you move to Connecticut too? Don't they have inns there?"

Melinda got to her feet and walked away. She certainly knew how to leave the bombshells until the end of the conversation. Sara hadn't thought of leaving Bluestar. It would take some thinking to see if she was up for something this major.

Bluestar had always been her home. This was where her family was. She halted her thoughts. What family? Her parents were gone. Her sister had moved halfway around the world and wasn't moving back. Not even Oreo was with her. Maybe her ties to Bluestar weren't as strong as she wanted to believe.

Chapter Twenty-One

I T WAS TIME TO talk to his parents.

Saturday afternoon, Kent went to their place. He knew his mother wouldn't take the news of him moving very well, but with time she'd adjust to the idea. He hoped.

He let himself in the front door, which was always unlocked. The front of the house was quiet, but there were voices coming from the kitchen, and there was laughter. His mother was happy?

He moved to the kitchen doorway and spotted his aunt Carol. He hadn't seen her since last summer. She lived in Ohio. She was his mother's sister and his favorite aunt. His aunt liked to say that she was a change of life baby—meaning she was a surprise that came along much later in his grandparents' lives. He chose not to give that idea too much thought.

Just then his aunt glanced up and noticed him standing there. "Kent."

She rushed over and gave him a hug. He glanced over his aunt's shoulder to see his mother still smiling.

His aunt pulled back and smiled up at him. "I think you're taller than the last time I saw you."

"I don't think so." He was way past that age.

"Oh. I guess this means I'm shrinking." She let out a laugh.

He loved that his aunt could make light-hearted jokes and laugh at herself. She never seemed to take life too seriously—except for when her husband died. Kent had never witnessed his aunt so distraught.

"And what brings you to Bluestar?" He couldn't remember his mother mentioning that his aunt was coming for a visit.

"I've made a decision. I'm moving here." Aunt Carol smiled brightly.

"Wow!" He hadn't anticipated her response. "That's wonderful. When?"

"Right now. I packed up my things and sold the house to a friend."

He swallowed hard. His aunt certainly didn't waste any time when she made up her mind to do something. It made him wonder why he was still waffling about taking the job on the mainland. His thoughts drifted to Sara. And then he pushed his troubles to the back of his mind.

He glanced at his mother, who was peeling a cooked potato to toss into a bowl for her famous potato salad. "Did you know about this?"

His mother shook her head. "It's all a surprise to me. I tried to call you this morning but your phone keeps going to voicemail."

"Really?" He pulled his phone from his pocket. When he tapped the screen, nothing happened. His finger pressed on a button on the side of the phone with no success. His phone was dead. "I must have forgotten to charge it last night."

His mother nodded in understanding. "I've been trying to figure out a place for your aunt to live. The vacant apartment above the store is spoken for, right?"

She meant the apartment Cari Chen was supposed to rent. "Actually, it just became available again."

Both of their faces lit up. It was strange how things worked out sometimes. He was happy for his aunt. He knew his mother had wanted this to happen since Aunt Carol's husband passed away a few years ago.

"So what brings you by?" his mother asked. "I thought you'd be off getting more people to sign up for your refresh service."

"His what?" Aunt Carol sat down at the kitchen island.

"It's what he calls his new decorating service," his mother said to his aunt before sending him an expectant look.

He swallowed hard and then uttered, "I've received a job offer in Connecticut."

Aunt Carol gaped while the potato slipped from his mother's hand. She lunged for it and caught it before it slid off the counter. She turned to him with a frown on her face. "Are congratulations in order?"

This was it. This was the moment he had to make a decision. "Yes."

It felt good to stop waffling back and forth between staying and going. But the decision didn't fill him with the happiness that he'd anticipated when he'd set off on this job search.

"Congratulations." Aunt Carol rushed over and gave him another quick hug. "This is wonderful. You'll have to tell me all about it."

"I will but I can't stay." His gaze returned to his mother, who was busy chopping the potato. His mother needed time to absorb the news, and then he'd talk to both of his parents at once. "I just wanted you to know."

His mother paused. Her hands rested on the edge of the mixing bowl with a paring knife in one hand and a chunk of potato in the other. "We're having a backyard picnic this evening. We invited some friends. You should bring Sara."

It didn't surprise him to hear that his mother was throwing an impromptu party. His mother was always looking for a reason to get people together. And normally he'd be down for it, especially with Aunt Carol on the island, but there would be questions—lots of questions—and he was running short on answers.

He cleared his throat. "I don't know. Sara might already have plans. I should be going."

"Kent," his mother called out. "Don't make any final decisions about the job. Your father and I would like a chance to speak to you about it."

"I think we said everything we had to say."

"No, we didn't. Just give us a chance. In the meantime, why don't you take your aunt to see the work you did at the inn?"

"If now isn't a good time," his aunt said, "I totally understand. But I can't wait to see what you did with the lobby." She clasped her hands together as she smiled at him. "Your mother has been talking about it since I got here."

The last thing he wanted to do was to run into Sara. As he saw the excitement written all over his aunt's face, he felt his resolve diminishing. After all, Bluestar was a small island, so he had to get used to running into Sara—even after he moved to Connecticut, he'd still come home to visit. It might be awkward at first, but he hoped with time they could move past it. He knew they'd never be close again, but he hoped there wouldn't be any animosity.

He looked at his aunt. "Okay. Let's go."

Aunt Carol told his mother she wouldn't be gone long and she'd help with the preparations for the picnic when she got back. And they set off. Aunt Carol told him about her decision to move to the island and how she lucked out in knowing someone who knew someone who was looking for a house.

When they reached the inn, he kept glancing around, expecting to see Sara. Each time he was disappointed. As he held the door to the lobby for his aunt, he spotted someone inside with a short dark bob just like Sara's hair. His heart beat faster. He wasn't sure what to say to her. As he followed his aunt inside, his mouth grew dry and his palms became damp. He rubbed his hands on his shorts.

The woman turned around. It wasn't Sara. Disappointment slammed into him. He tried to tell himself it was for the best. After all, what was left to say? Come Monday morning, he'd be calling the company in Hartford and letting them know he was accepting the position.

"This is beautiful." Aunt Carol's voice drew him from his meandering thoughts.

"You don't have to be nice."

She turned to look at him. "I'm not. This is really nice. You have a really good eye."

"I can't take all of the credit. Sara helped me a lot. It was a team effort."

"This Sara I keep hearing about, is she your girlfriend?"

Heat scorched his face, as though he'd been lying on the beach all day without any sunscreen. "No."

His aunt studied him for a moment. "But you'd like her to be, wouldn't you?"

"Shh..." He glanced around to make sure no one had overheard their conversation. "If you're going to live in Bluestar, you have to know that whatever is said in public becomes part of the town's gossip."

His aunt smiled. "I didn't think about that. I'll keep it in mind going forward."

"I thought I saw a familiar face." Harvey made his way over to them with a welcoming smile. "Thank you, Kent, for all of your hard work. Everyone loves what you and Sara have done with the lobby."

"I certainly do too," Aunt Carol said.

Harvey turned to his aunt. "And who is this beautiful young woman?"

Kent noticed the blush that came over his aunt. He made the formal introduction between the two. He wasn't sure if they'd met before on one of his aunt's visits or not. He watched as Harvey took his aunt's hand in his and shook it. All the while they gazed into each other's eyes.

"Are you staying on the island for long?" Harvey asked his aunt.

"Actually, I'm moving here."

"That's wonderful. If you need someone to show you around the island, I'd be more than happy to offer my services."

Was Harvey flirting with his aunt? Kent's gaze moved back and forth between the two of them. They hadn't taken their eyes off of each other.

"Why I'd like that very much," Aunt Carol said.

Kent didn't understand. His aunt knew her way around the island. She'd been coming to the island for years and spending summer vacations here. But something told him she wasn't looking for a tour guide as much as some companionship. And Harvey was a widower, whom Sara said was starting to date again.

Suddenly, Kent felt like a third wheel. He glanced around once more for Sara to get him out of this awkward situation. As Harvey and his aunt spoke, it was as if they'd forgotten he was even there.

Maybe it was best he make an excuse to leave because he was obviously not needed here. Besides, his aunt knew her way back to his parents' place.

Kent pulled out his phone and stared at the black screen. "Aunt Carol, I just got a message. Something came up and I need to take care of it. Will you be all right on your own?"

Never taking her gaze off of Harvey, she said, "I'll be perfectly fine."

"I'll see to it," Harvey said.

Okay then. He was obviously no longer needed. "I'll see you later."

"Kent," his aunt called out, "don't forget to charge your phone. It makes it easier to get messages."

Ouch! He'd been totally busted. This time it was the heat of embarrassment that stung his cheeks. He watched as Harvey guided his aunt around the room. Kent walked out the door with no destination in mind. His social life wasn't going nearly as well as his aunt's.

CHAPTER TWENTY-TWO

WHY WASN'T HE ANSWERING?

Sara disconnected her call to Kent. She inwardly groaned in frustration. Was he ducking her? Probably. It would serve her right if he was after brushing him off last night.

But things looked much different in the light of day. She'd done a lot of thinking since her conversation with Melinda. In fact, it was all she'd thought about. At first, the thought of leaving Bluestar was utterly daunting, but the more she really thought of it, the more she realized that without her family, there was no reason she couldn't start over somewhere else.

Although she knew without a doubt she'd never get an apartment as amazing as her current one with its most spectacular view of the ocean. Still, it was a small sacrifice for her to be with Kent.

She'd even started to research some job opportunities in Hartford, as well as places to live. She'd flagged a couple of job postings that held some interest. She could always take a temporary position until she found something more to her taste.

Now that she'd come around to the idea of moving, she needed to talk to Kent. But every time she called him, it went straight to his voicemail. She thought of leaving him a message, but she needed to have this conversation in person.

She went to his apartment and knocked on the door. A neighbor happened by and let her know he'd left earlier and hadn't been spotted since. She thanked the older woman.

Where was he? Did he already leave the island? Impossible. Nobody moves that quickly. He was somewhere in Bluestar. She just had to find him so they could talk.

Maybe he went to work at his family's store. It sounded like a plausible idea—at least that was what she hoped. It was only a couple of blocks to Turner Furniture.

The building looked exactly as it had all of her life. Even the layout in the store was the same. She could see why Kent was anxious to make some changes. Either you changed or you became stagnant. Luckily, the Turners had a monopoly on the island as they were the only furniture store.

It wasn't a bad-looking place with its red brick exterior and its huge picture windows with various room setups. The furniture was nice—more of a traditional style. She could see places where Kent could make some changes. The modifications didn't have to encompass the entire store. Perhaps adding some more modern pieces here and there for the younger generation would help. Maybe some gaming chairs for people like his brother Owen, who liked to spend a bunch of time in the virtual world.

Her heart raced as she entered the store. The last time she'd sought him out here, things hadn't gone well. In fact, they hadn't spoken for a long time after that scene.

Today would be different. There would be no harsh words exchanged. Although she wasn't sure how Kent was going to take her news. Would he be happy and pull her into his arms? Or would he say it was too late? Had she messed things up permanently?

"Hi, Sara." Kent's father moved toward her. "How can I help you?" He gestured to some furniture to his left. "We have some pieces on sale over here?"

She glanced at the white and blue upholstered living room set. "They're very nice, but I'm not here to shop."

"Oh... You're here to see Kent."

She nodded. "I am. Is he around?"

"I'm afraid not. And I don't know where he is, but we're having a picnic at the house in a little bit. You should join us." When she hesitated, he said, "Kent will be there. His aunt is moving to Bluestar. Our family and friends are getting together to welcome her. In fact, I was just going to close the store a little early. I have one stop to make on the way home, but you're welcome to go on ahead."

It sounded like a family affair. She didn't want to crash their party. And her talk with Kent wasn't appropriate for an audience.

"Thank you so much for the invitation, but I have some other plans."

"That's too bad. I know my wife will be disappointed."

"Have a good time." She turned for the door.

"I'll tell Kent you were looking for him."

She turned back. "Thanks. I'd appreciate it."

And that was it. She was out of ideas. For all she knew he could be at a friend's or at one of his brother's places. There were too many places he could be. She wasn't going to run all around the island, trying to track him down. Maybe this was a sign. And not a good one.

This wasn't going to be easy.

Kent had the day to get used to his decision to leave Bluestar. There was a lot to be excited about with this new journey, but there was still a part of him that felt like he was leaving a lot behind. But he wasn't going to change his mind. He couldn't go back to the way things had been for years and would remain for who knew how long.

But tonight he would focus on the backyard party at his parents' house. With a box of baked goods from The Elegant Bakery, Kent stepped into his parents' house. He could hear voices coming from the kitchen. He stepped into the room and saw his mother working side by side with her sister as they prepped the food.

He held out the white bakery box. "I brought this. I figured these cookies would be better than anything I could ever come up with."

His mother smiled. "Thank you. But you know you didn't have to bring anything."

"Yes, I did. You shouldn't have to take care of everything."

"You are such a sweetheart." His mother beamed at him.

"Someone raised him right," his aunt chimed in.

He opened the box and placed it on the kitchen island. He wasn't sure if his mother would serve the cookies in the box or want to put them on a tray. It was hard to tell with his mother. Sometimes she was informal, and other times she liked things to look proper.

"I'm not late, am I?" the familiar voice came from behind him.

Kent turned to find his father entering the kitchen. He had a white envelope in his hand. Must be some mail from the store. He'd normally ask if it was something he had to deal with but he stopped himself. He had to start disengaging from the family business. In two weeks, he'd be gone, and his parents would have to handle whatever came up. It was going to take some time for them to get used to this new arrangement.

"You're right on time," his mother said.

His father turned to him. "We have something to discuss."

Kent shook his head. "Not tonight. This is supposed to be a celebration."

"Yes, tonight," his father said firmly. "This won't wait."

"I'm going to take these delicious cookies outside." His aunt scooped up the bakery box and made her way to the backyard.

When they were alone, his mother turned to his father. "Did you get it?"

He nodded. "I have it right here." He held up the envelope. "Do you want to tell him?"

His mother wiped her hands off on a towel and then stepped around the island. "Your father and I have been doing some serious talking."

"Mom, you don't have to do this." He knew they were going to say anything to change his mind, and he knew once he agreed to stay on that things would go back to the way they had been.

"You hush now." His mother frowned at him. "Your father and I have decided that we aren't ready to retire. I just can't imagine us sitting around the house all day. The store has been our life for so many years."

"I understand. And that's why I need to take this new job," Kent said.

His father cleared his throat. "What you didn't give your mother a chance to say is that even though we aren't prepared to turn our backs on the business, we do want more flexibility in our schedules. We have a lot of traveling we want to do, and for one reason or another, we could never do it before. But now is our time to see the country and maybe more."

His mother slipped her hand into his father's. "We trust you. We think you'll do an amazing job running the business."

"Even if I make changes?"

His parents hesitated but then nodded their heads. His mother said, "We loved your refresh idea. We'd like to see you run with it."

They were saying all of the right things, but this wasn't the first time his parents said these sorts of things. It just wasn't enough this time. He was getting too old now to keep wishing things would change.

As though his mother could read his mind, she said, "George, give him the envelope."

His father held out the envelope to him. When Kent took it, he saw the name of a local attorney. "What's this?"

"Open it," his mother said.

What had they done? He ripped open the envelope. When he pulled out the papers, he unfolded them to find it was some sort of a contract between himself and his parents. His gaze lifted to them. "What is this?"

"It's a formal agreement between the three of us," his father said. "We want you to feel that you have an equal voice in the business, and this lays it all out."

Wow! His parents had never gone to this extreme before. They must really be worried that he was leaving.

"So will you stay?" His mother's eyes reflected her hope.

He glanced down over the agreement, giving him control over the day-to-day operation and expansion. It was everything he'd been asking for. Except if he was running the business, he wouldn't have time to implement the refresh project.

"There is one thing," Kent said.

"What's that?" his mother asked. "I'm sure we can work it out."

"It's the refresh project. I can't execute it and take care of the business."

"Excuse me." His aunt stepped into the kitchen. "The grill is hot, and Liam asked for the burgers." She moved toward the refrigerator.

"I have an idea." His mother's eyes twinkled as though she were up to something. "Hey Carol, are you looking for a job?"

His aunt's brows rose. "I plan to job hunt as soon as I get settled."

Kent knew what his mother was up to. His aunt had a flair for decorating. She would be a natural at the refresh project.

"How would you feel about taking on the refresh service for the store?"

"Me?" Aunt Carol pressed a hand to her chest. "I don't know. I mean this is Kent's idea."

"If I'm managing the store," Kent said, "I won't have time to take on refresh projects. So, we'll need to hire someone. If you're available, the job is yours."

Aunt Carol was hesitant. "I'll give it a try. I don't know if I can do it as well as you."

"I already know you can do better," Kent said. "And I have your first project. The Seaside Bookshop."

"So it's all settled?" his mother asked.

"Not quite," his father said. "We have to sign the agreement."

His parents signed first, and then his mother handed Kent the pen. He glanced up at them. "Are you both sure you're ready to do this?" When both of his parents nodded, he signed the contract.

His father gathered the papers. "I'll have copies made for us. And Kent, I almost forgot, Sara was looking for you a little bit ago. She looked really disappointed that you weren't at the store. I invited her to the picnic, but she turned me down."

"Sara?" His mind started spinning. There was so much he needed to tell her. And he didn't feel it could wait. He looked at his aunt. "I know this is your party, but would you mind if I stepped out for a bit? This is really important."

"I would never stand in the way of love. Go get her." His aunt smiled.

He didn't need to be told twice. He turned and headed for the door. He pulled it open and practically ran into Harvey. What was he doing there? Kent couldn't remember his parents inviting Harvey to one of their backyard parties.

"Hey, Kent." Harvey sent him a friendly smile. "I hope you don't mind that I stopped by. Your aunt mentioned the party and said I should stop by."

Ah... Now it all made sense. "It's good to see you. I think you'll find Aunt Carol in the kitchen." He pointed in the direction. "I just have to step out for a bit."

After Harvey stepped inside, Kent rushed out the door. He had to find Sara. They had a lot of talking to do.

CHAPTER TWENTY-THREE

Tonight was the Concert on the Beach.

Sara moved restlessly around her apartment. She was so bored she'd baked some apricot blondie bars. Originally, she'd sought out the recipe to bake for Kent, but they'd gotten so busy with the lobby she'd forgotten about the recipe...until now.

The pan was in the oven at the moment. She inhaled deeply, savoring the sweet buttery aroma. While she waited, she'd gotten out a dust rag and was spiffing up the living room. This was by far the worst vacation she'd ever taken.

Usually, she got together with some friends, and they planned a trip somewhere. Once it was to New York City for a week of Broadway shows. Another time it was to New Orleans for Mardi Gras. And another time it was a trip to California to see the giant redwood trees.

This time she'd been planning to help her sister get settled into her new apartment on the island, but that had fallen through. She thought of calling Cari, but she wasn't sure what to say. She was still hurting from her sister's sudden change of mind. Sure, she'd get over it.

After all, they were family, but it just might take her a moment or two.

And so she was left home alone without her sister, without Oreo, and most of all, without Kent. She was definitely doing something wrong. Maybe she should try calling Kent again. She grabbed her phone from the kitchen counter and dialed his number. It once more went to voicemail. What was wrong with him? Didn't he ever charge his phone? She sighed.

Ding.

The blondies were done. She moved to the kitchen. With a hot mitt, she pulled the pan from the oven and placed it on a hot pad to cool. She inhaled the sweet aroma. It smelled so good. She couldn't wait to have some, but it would be a while until it cooled.

She glanced at the clock. It was almost seven o'clock. This was the time she'd agreed to meet Kent at the concert. She wondered if he remembered about their date? She doubted it. He had a lot on his mind now that he had the job in Hartford.

But with the living room dusted, the vacuum run in every room, the bathroom spiffed up and a load of laundry washed, dried, and put away, there was nothing left to do in her apartment. So she changed her clothes, put on some makeup, and headed to the concert alone.

She would undoubtedly run into someone she knew, probably a lot of people she knew. Just not the one person she wanted to see.

The last of the sun's rays warmed her skin as she made her way to Beachcomber Park. Music from the concert filled the air. It was so loud she could barely hear herself think. She immediately recognized the female voice. The song was one they played regularly on Bluestar's radio station. It was their very own country star, Em Bell. She sounded amazing.

Sara loved how even though Em was a huge star now with a couple of number one hits, she still made time for the people of Bluestar. And it wasn't just performing. Em still participated in as many of the island's functions as her schedule permitted.

There were a lot of people in the park. Some were there for a walk. Some had their children playing on the playground equipment. A young mother pushed her son on a swing. Sara kept walking.

When she glanced up, she realized she'd come to a stop in front of the sandcastle sculpture, the spot where she'd agreed to meet Kent. She glanced at the time on her fitness watch. It was a couple of minutes after seven. She couldn't resist looking to see if Kent was around. She didn't see him.

There was a bench nearby. She sat down. She thought about pulling up a digital book on her phone. While she preferred paperbacks, she would occasionally read on her phone. But the music was so loud she'd never be able to focus on reading. It didn't stop her from mindlessly scrolling through her social media.

"Is this seat taken?" the male voice called out over the music.

She glanced up. Her gaze collided with Kent's. Her heart leapt into her throat. He'd come. He'd remembered. Not trusting her voice, she nodded.

He sat down next to her. He practically had to shout to be heard. "Can we talk?"

"What?" Even with him yelling she was having a hard time hearing him. "I can't hear you."

"Can we talk!?"

She once more nodded. "Not here!"

She got to her feet and gestured for him to follow her. He did. They walked to the far end of the park and then crossed the road and headed down to the beach.

When the music receded into the background, she said, "I've been trying to reach you."

"We need to talk."

"I thought that's what we were doing." She sent him a tentative smile, hoping to lighten the mood.

He smiled back. "I see how it's going to be. But seriously, I have some stuff I need to tell you."

"I have something to tell you too. Can I go first?" She pleaded with her eyes.

"Do you really think those puppy dog eyes are going to work on me?"

Her smile broadened. "I don't know. You tell me."

He sighed. "Go ahead."

"You know I've been trying to call you all day."

"I'm sorry. My phone died last night after searching for Oreo, and I forgot to put it on the charger."

"So, you weren't trying to avoid me?"

"Definitely not. But you were pretty emphatic when you told me to leave last night."

"I'm really sorry about that." If she wanted him to be honest with her, she would have to be brutally honest with him. It would mean letting down her guard and making herself vulnerable. "I was afraid of being hurt so...I pushed you away."

"And you're not afraid of that today?"

She shook her head. "I've learned a lot since then. A good friend of mine talked some sense into me."

"They did, huh? And what did you learn?"

"Well, this morning I did an internet search of the hotels and inns in Hartford." The breath caught in her throat as she waited for his response. She hoped he'd be surprised and happy about the idea.

"Why would you do that?"

It was not the response she'd anticipated. "Because I'm moving there." She stopped walking and turned to him. "What we have is too special to lose." She drew in a deep breath and let it out. "Kent, I love you."

His eyes momentarily widened. "I love you too."

He drew her close to him. Her palms came to rest on his muscled chest. Her heart was pounding so loud it echoed in her ears. She wondered if he could hear it.

He loved her. He loved her. He loved her.

The very special words repeated over and over in her mind. Her heart was so full of love now that it felt as though it were going to burst. This was the best day of her life.

His gaze dipped to her lips. He was going to kiss her, and she couldn't think of anything she'd like better. She lifted up on her tiptoes as she looped her arms around his neck. And then she pulled him toward her. When his lips touched hers, her heart pitter-pattered.

She didn't care what it took; they would find a middle ground so they could be together. She was tired of losing the people she loved from her life. With her parents, it was beyond her control. With her sister, it was her sister's choice. With Oreo, she couldn't stop it. But with Kent, there was a will and there was a way. Hartford here she comes.

When they pulled away, he stared deep into her eyes. "I'm so sorry about all of what happened. I never meant to hurt you."

"And I'm sorry for pushing you away. I don't want to push you away anymore. I want to pull you close—very close." She lifted up on her toes and pressed a quick kiss to his lips.

"Mm... I like being close to you too." He smiled at her. "But you don't have to move."

"Yes, I do. We aren't going to try a long-distance relationship. It just won't work."

"No. I mean you don't have to move because I'm not leaving."

"You're not?" She was confused. "Why? What happened?"

He told her about the job offer in Hartford and how he'd told his parents. He told her about the contract his parents had drawn up. "And that's why I'm not leaving Bluestar."

Her gaze searched his. "Are you sure this is what you want?"

He nodded his head. "This is everything I've wanted. Bluestar is my home. I hope it will always be my home—with you." He stared deep into her eyes. "I've never loved someone like I love you."

"I love you too."

CHAPTER TWENTY-FOUR

H E WAS SO HAPPY.

She was so happy.

At last it was going to work out.

Before Kent could kiss her again, her phone started to ring. Talk about lousy timing. He restrained a sigh when she pulled away to answer the call.

Not much was said on her end. There was a lot of *uh-huhs* and *yeses*. He was left to wonder who was on the other end of the conversation.

When tears splashed onto her cheeks, fear settled in his chest. It was all he could do not to rip the phone out of her hands and find out who was making her cry. But then she smiled at him through her tears and the knot of fear eased.

A few moments later Sara disconnected the call. "It was the Watsons. They wanted to know if I wanted to keep Oreo."

"What did you tell them?"

"Of course I said yes." More happy tears spilled onto her cheeks.

He reached out and pulled her into his arms. He enjoyed holding her close. They were like two puzzle pieces that fit perfectly together.

When Sara pulled away, she said, "They'll be here soon. I can't believe this day."

"Let's go."

Hand-in-hand they made their way to Sara's apartment. She was so excited she was practically dragging him behind her. He loved seeing her this excited.

Once they were in her apartment, he said, "This day has been pretty remarkable."

"It's amazing. I'll have both of my guys back in my life."

"Wait. Are you saying I'm in competition with Oreo?"

"Of course not. He's my furbaby." She leaned in close to him. "You're my guy. And you get these." She kissed him.

He would never get tired of her sweet kisses. How did he get to be so lucky? "Is that all I get?"

She pulled away and moved to the kitchen, where she produced a tray of sweets. "No. You can have some of these blondie bars."

"Count me in." He didn't care what was in them. He would enjoy them just because Sara baked them. "So you're going to bake for me all of the time?" He teased her.

"Hey, I have a job too. I don't have time to mess up the kitchen all of the time. But if you're nice to me, we'll see if I can manage them every now and then."

He took a bite and moaned in pleasure. They were, in fact, delicious. He loved the flavorful bits of apricots and the bits of pecans. He had no idea Sara could bake, but she was very talented.

Knock-knock.

"It must be the Watsons." Sara rushed around the kitchen island and practically ran to the door. She swung it open with a big smile on her face. "Hi. Please come in."

Kent stood back and took it all in. Mr. Watson looked a bit disgruntled, and his wife looked frazzled. Obviously, Oreo hadn't been happy about being taken away from Sara, not that Kent could blame the little guy.

"We're sorry to do this," Mrs. Watson said. "It's just since we took Oreo home, he has been throwing a fit. He cries all of the time. He's constantly trying to run out the door. And he won't eat. We took him to the vet, who couldn't find anything wrong with him."

Sara's gaze moved to the carrier with Oreo staring out at her. "Do you mind if I let him out?"

Mrs. Watson shook her head. "Go ahead."

Kent quietly observed. He was surprised Sara wasn't bouncing up and down with joy to have Oreo back. He knew how much she loved and missed Oreo. And yet she was acting so calm and reserved.

Sara let Oreo out of the carrier. The little kitty strutted right out of the carrier. He stopped and looked around as though figuring out where he was. Then he ran over to Sara and rubbed over her ankles. His purr was heard by all.

"I can't believe this," Mrs. Watson said. "He didn't act like this with us."

Sara obviously didn't know what to say, so she said nothing at all.

"It's obvious he has chosen you to be his human." Mr. Watson held up two store bags. "We bought some kitten supplies."

"Thank you." Sara bent down and picked up Oreo, who continued to purr and rub over her jawline. "How much do I owe you?"

"Nothing at all." Mr. Watson smiled. "You've already done a lot by taking in the kitten."

She moved to the kitchen and got the kitten some food. Oreo immediately wolfed down the wet food as though he hadn't eaten in a week. It was obvious to everyone in the room that Oreo was happy with Sara. They belonged together.

After the Watsons left, Sara squealed with joy as she jumped up and down. Now this was the reaction he'd been expecting. A smile pulled at Kent's lips as he watched her do a happy dance.

When she calmed down, she looked at him. "What are you smiling at?"

"You. Are you happy?"

She moved to him and wrapped her arms around his neck. "I'm delightfully happy. Thanks to my two guys."

"I think your other guy wore himself out."

"Why do you say that?"

He nodded toward the couch. Sara released her hold on him to turn around. Oreo was curled up in the middle of the couch sound asleep.

"Aw... Isn't he the cutest?" Sara crooned.

"Hey, what about me?" Kent feigned a pout.

She turned around and once more looped her arms around his neck. She sent him a teasing grin. "You're not so bad either."

And then she pressed a kiss to his lips. His heart filled with love. He'd definitely found a keeper. He had a feeling their future would be full of twists and turns but as long as they had each other, there wasn't anything they couldn't face together.

She couldn't quit smiling.

Later that evening, she was curled up with Kent and Oreo on the couch, watching a rom-com that she'd talked Kent into watching with her. She'd even popped some popcorn for the occasion.

Their shoulders were touching, and their hands were clasped with their fingers laced. She could definitely get used to this. On her lap, Oreo had taken up residence. Every now and then he'd stretch, blow out a breath, and then go back to sleep. When she ran a hand over his baby soft fur, he let out his loud purr.

If she was dreaming, she never wanted to wake up. This was more than she could ever hope for. If only her sister was on the island, it would make everything perfect, but she understood that her sister had to find her own path in life.

Sara glanced over at Kent just as he glanced over at her. She smiled, and then he smiled. Her heart pitter-pattered.

"Are you happy?" she asked.

"Very much so."

She sank down on the couch cushions and placed her head on his muscled shoulder before tossing another buttery piece of popcorn into her mouth. This was just the first of many evenings of contented bliss.

Buzz-buzz.

She sighed. It was her phone, and it was across the room on the kitchen island. Why hadn't she brought it over to the couch? She glanced at Oreo, who looked utterly content. She hated to move him. Maybe she'd let it go to voicemail. But she worried it might be something about the inn.

As though reading her mind, Kent said, "I'll grab it for you."

"Thank you. And Oreo thanks you too."

"I think Oreo is going to be one spoiled kitten."

Sara grinned. "Is there a problem with that?"

"Not if it makes you happy."

"Good answer."

He handed her the phone. She glanced at the caller ID and was surprised to see it was the Brass Anchor Inn. "It's my work. They never call at this hour."

She pressed the phone to her ear. "Hello."

"Sara, I'm sorry to bother you." It was Harvey. His breathing was labored, and his voice sounded off. "I'm not feeling so well. I was hoping you could finish my shift."

"Certainly." She knew Harvey well enough to know he wasn't a complainer. In fact, he was quite the opposite. This must be serious. "I'll be right there. Harvey?"

The line went dead.

"What's wrong?" Concern laced Kent's voice.

"It was Harvey. He said he doesn't feel well. He wants me to finish his shift, and then the line went dead. This isn't like him. I'm worried."

Kent got to his feet. "Let's go."

She gently placed Oreo on the couch. He murred at her before he went back to sleep. She jumped to her feet, grabbed her purse from the counter, and followed Kent out the door.

Hand in hand they rushed to the inn. They didn't talk much, each lost in their own thoughts. In the background, the concert was still going on.

When they reached the inn, they entered the lobby. No one was there. It wasn't uncommon at this late hour. She moved down the hallway to Harvey's office.

"Harvey?" She stepped around the corner and gasped.

Harvey was collapsed on the floor next to his desk. Her heart lurched into her throat. *No-no. This can't be happening.* He had to be all right.

She rushed toward him. Kent was right behind her.

"Help me roll him over," Kent said.

They moved Harvey as gently as they could. And then Kent checked for a pulse. While he started CPR, she called 911. It was all a blur from there as she communicated between Kent and the 911 operator.

It seemed like forever until the paramedics arrived—even though it was just a matter of minutes. Kent's younger brother Liam was one of the paramedics. He was as tall as his older brother and almost as good-looking. Though there was a guarded look in Liam's eyes that wasn't there with Kent. Maybe it had something to do with Liam's divorce. She knew it hadn't been easy on him.

But he was an amazing father. Everybody in town loved when Liam brought his three-year-old son, Tate, to The Lighthouse Café. The residents would stop by their table and ooh and awe over Tate. She didn't, but it didn't mean she hadn't been tempted. When Liam was with his son, he always looked so happy.

Tonight Liam's face was creased with worry lines. He was all business as he moved in and took over the CPR for his brother. Kent moved to Sara's side and draped an arm over her shoulders, pulling her in close for a hug. A tight hug. For a moment, they clung to each other as they attempted to come to terms with this serious situation.

With the ambulance's siren wailing and red lights flashing, they transported Harvey to the island's medical center. This wasn't good. Not good at all.

As they stood in the parking lot, Sara turned to Kent, whose face was creased with worry lines. "I need to stay here. You... You should go to the medical center. I... I'll try to get ahold of his daughter and let Josie know."

Kent looked at her with concern in his eyes. "Are you going to be okay?"

She swallowed hard and nodded. "I've got this. Just go make sure Harvey is okay. He just has to be."

She couldn't imagine life without Harvey's big smiles or his bear hugs. He was such a good guy and so full of life. They just couldn't lose him. She banished the thought. It wasn't going to happen. He would be fine.

Kent lifted her chin until they were staring into each other's eyes. It was in his steady gaze that she found the strength she needed to get through this evening. Kent lowered his head and gave her a tender kiss.

He pulled back. "Try not to worry too much. He's in good hands. We'll get through this together."

She blinked repeatedly and nodded. "Take one of the inn's carts. She ran inside, grabbed a key, and rushed back out. She handed him the key. His fingers caught hers and held on. "Go."

With reluctance he let her hand go and then walked away.

With the wail of the siren in the distance, she reached for her phone. It was time to make the dreaded phone call. No one ever wanted to make this call. And no one ever wanted to receive this call. She'd been on the receiving end of such a call, and it had torn her heart out. With a shaky finger, she called Melinda.

Continue reading Harvey's story in A Seaside Bookshop Christmas. Join Melinda, Liam and Harvey for a very special holiday!

Epilogue

Bluestar Island, Christmas Eve...

C HRISTMAS WISHES DO COME true.

Sara couldn't stop smiling. Her cheeks ached, but she kept grinning. Santa had come early that year.

Ever since the Concert on the Beach, she'd spent almost every free moment with Kent. Of course, their calendars didn't always sync up because of their work schedules, but they did the best they could to see each other every day, even if it was just for a quick coffee at The Lighthouse Café.

Sometimes they went on adventures around the island. Other times they would venture to the mainland. For his birthday, she'd surprised him with football tickets, and so they'd spent a long weekend in Foxborough, Massachusetts. For her birthday, he'd given her a spa weekend. It had been absolutely fabulous. Other than those two extravagances, they'd been saving their money. They both knew they were destined to have a future together.

Her sister and new husband had flown in for the holidays—talk about an amazing gift—to spend time with Cari. They'd gone caroling and returned to have a lasagna dinner with sides. With the fireplace lit and the glow of the Christmas tree, they'd enjoyed a leisurely dinner. There had been lots of laughter and a few trips down memory lane.

Time had flown by, and now with the dishes cleaned and put away, the evening was winding down. Sara didn't want it to end.

"Thank you for dinner." Cari hugged her.

"And thank you for helping with the cleanup." Sara smiled at her sister.

Cari nudged her sister and then nodded toward the guys on the couch with Oreo in between as they watched football on her big screen TV. "Looks like they have something in common."

"I have a feeling they'll be watching many more games together."

Cari nodded. "Me too. But we should get going. It's getting late, and tomorrow will be a big day."

"And another big meal." Not that Sara minded all of the cooking. She loved having her whole family together. Cooking for them was a pleasure. As for the clean-up, it wasn't so much of a pleasure, but she'd do it again and again if it meant having her loved ones in one room.

"Adam, it's time to go."

"Hang on one second. I just have to see if they make this kick."

A couple seconds later, there was cheering from the couch. Their team must have made the kick. There was another round of hugs followed by thank yous and then goodnights. Cari and Adam were off to the Brass Anchor Inn for the night.

Sara closed the door and turned to Kent. "It was a wonderful evening, wasn't it?"

He smiled at her. "I've never seen you so happy."

"I've never had all of my loved ones in one place. I can't imagine Christmas getting any better."

Kent arched a brow. "Are you sure?"

"I don't know. What do you have in mind?"

"I've been waiting all day to do this." He reached into his pocket and pulled out a black velvet box. He got down on one knee and opened it. A giant diamond solitaire twinkled at her. "Sara, you are my best friend. I can't imagine my life without you in it. I love you with all of my heart. Will you marry me?"

Tears of joy blurred her vision. "Yes. Yes, I will. I love you too."

Her hand trembled when he slid the ring onto her finger. It was a little big, but it didn't matter to her. All that mattered was that he loved her and she loved him. The rest of it they'd work out.

He straightened and pulled her into his arms. She was staring at the sparkling ring as he drew her closer. Her hand pressed to his chest.

She lifted her gaze to meet his. "Only you could take a perfect evening and make it even better."

He pressed a kiss to her lips. She was the luckiest woman in the world. Just wait until she told her sister. But as Kent deepened the kiss, she realized that announcing their engagement could most definitely wait.

"*Meow.*"

Cat claws dug at her pants. She grudgingly pulled away from Kent and glanced down to see Oreo leaning against her leg.

She bent down and picked him up. He'd grown a lot over the past six months. He was no longer a little kitty. He was now long and lanky.

"*Meow.*"

Kent pet Oreo's head. "What's the matter, buddy? Are you jealous? Afraid I'm going to take up too much of your mom's time?"

She hugged Oreo, who let out one of his loud purrs that sounded more like the rev of a small engine. "Don't worry. I have enough love and time for both of you."

Kent draped an arm over her shoulders. "I can't wait to make our family official."

"Me either. What about a spring wedding?"

"I don't know. Can you make arrangements that fast?"

"I don't want anything fancy. Although I do want my sister there."

"I understand. You talk to her and see when she can come back. All you have to do is give me a date, and I'll be there." He leaned over and pressed a kiss to her lips.

Keep reading Sara and Kent's story! Sign up for my newsletter and receive a Bonus Epilogue.

Get your bonus epilogue HERE.

And then return to Bluestar Island for the next book in this heartwarming series...A SEASIDE BOOKSHOP CHRISTMAS. This snowy Christmas a bookshop owner, who is about to risk everything for her family, and a single dad is in over his head must

rely on each other this holiday season to keep their lives from imploding.

Sara's Apricot Blondies

Sara's Apricot Blondies (makes 12)

INGREDIENTS:

½ cup granulated sugar
½ cup light brown sugar
½ cup dark brown sugar
½ cup unsalted butter, melted
½ tsp baking powder
½ tsp salt
1 tsp vanilla
2 eggs
1 ½ cups flour
½ cup dried apricots, chopped
½ cup pecans, chopped

- Preheat oven to 350°F

- Grease and flour 9x13 pan.

- Combine butter, granulated, light and dark brown sugars. Mix.

- Add baking powder, salt, and vanilla. Mix.

- Add eggs. Mix.

- Slowly add remaining flour, a little at a time. Mix just until moistened.

- Add apricots and pecans. Stir by hand until combined.

- Bake for approximately 30 minutes or until toothpick inserted in center comes out clean.

- Enjoy.

Afterword

Thanks so much for reading Sara and Kent's story. I hope their journey made your heart smile. If you did enjoy the book, please consider...

- Help spreading the word about Summer Refresh by writing a review.
- Subscribe to my newsletter in order to receive information about my next release as well as find out about giveaways and special sales.
- You can like my author page on Facebook.

I hope you'll come back to Bluestar Island and read the continuing adventures of its residents.

Coming next is Melinda and Liam's story in A Seaside Bookshop Christmas.

Thanks again for your support! It is HUGELY appreciated.

Happy reading,
Jennifer

About Author

Award-winning author, Jennifer Faye pens fun, heartwarming contemporary romances with rugged cowboys, sexy billionaires and enchanting royalty. With more than a million books sold, she is internationally published with books translated into more than a dozen languages. She is a two-time winner of the RT Book Reviews Reviewers' Choice Award, the CataRomance Reviewers' Choice Award, named a TOP PICK author, and been nominated for numerous other awards.

Now living her dream, she resides with her very patient husband and two spoiled cats. When she's not plotting out her next romance, you can find her curled up with a mug of tea and a book. You can learn more about Jennifer at www.JenniferFaye.com

Subscribe to Jennifer's newsletter for news about upcoming releases, bonus content and other special offers.

You can also join her on Bookbub, Facebook, or Goodreads.

Made in the USA
Monee, IL
28 October 2025